THE SCANNER DIDN'T beep or buzz. It made no noise at all.

"Well?" Mott asked.

"No microchip, I'm afraid," Shelter Guy answered. "You found him in the recycling bin, you said?"

"Behind Mi-T-Mart. I was recycling my root beer bottle."

"Please don't eat my hand, little scruff." The pup was trying to get Shelter Guy's entire hand in his jaws.

"Do you know what kind of dog he is?" Mott asked.

Shelter Guy's frown dug even deeper. "Kid, this isn't a dog. This is a wolf."

Also by Greg van Eekhout

Voyage of the Dogs

Cog

Weird Kid

The Ghost Job

FENRIS & Mott

GREG VAN EEKHOUT

HARPER
An Imprint of HarperCollinsPublishers

Library of Congress Cataloging-in-Publication Data

Names: Van Eekhout, Greg, author.

Title: Fenris & Mott / Greg van Eekhout.

Other titles: Fenris and Mott

Description: First edition. | New York : Harper, [2022] | Audience: Ages 8–12. | Audience: Grades 4–6. | Summary: Mott's life becomes complicated when the abandoned puppy she found turns out to be a mythical Norse wolf who is partly responsible for bringing about the end of the worlds.

Identifiers: LCCN 2021057381 | ISBN 978-0-06-297064-0

Subjects: CYAC: Wolves—Fiction. | Mythology, Norse—Fiction. | End of the world—Fiction. | Fate and fatalism—Fiction. | Los Angeles (Calif.)—Fiction. | LCGFT: Novels.

Classification: LCC PZ7.V2744 Fe 2022 | DDC [Fic]—dc23

LC record available at https://lccn.loc.gov/2021057381

Typography by Chris Kwon

23 24 25 26 27   PC/CWR   10 9 8 7 6 5 4 3 2 1

First paperback edition, 2023

For Lisa Will, my loving bearer of shield and sword

✦ ✦ ✦

MOTT WAS RECORDING A ROOT BEER review video in the alley behind the Mi-T-Mart when she found the puppy.

Holding her phone in one hand and an open bottle of root beer in the other, she put on a big smile and thumbed the Record button.

"Hi, fellow Bubble Heads, it's another episode of the Mott and Amanda Root Beer Show! As you can see, the show's a little different today. For one thing, I'm flying solo since Amanda's on vacation with her family in Germany and they wouldn't spring for an expensive phone plan, so she can't do videos right now. In fact, she's hardly even messaging me. That's right, I haven't heard from my best friend in more than a week. But that's okay! I'm doing fine on my own! Another difference is that I'm not even in Pennsylvania anymore on account of me and my mom moving all the way out to Culver City, California. That's near Los Angeles, literally thousands of miles from Amanda. So I'm not recording this in Amanda's kitchen like you're used to seeing, with the restaurant-quality stove and the good lighting and the quiet neighbors. It's just me, by myself, in an alley with traffic noise and pigeons. And a sort of rancid odor, and . . . and . . . this is just pathetic."

She pressed the Stop button and deleted the video without even watching it. This was her third attempt at recording a review on her own, each one worse than the last. She'd tried inside the new apartment, but you could hear the neighbors' loud music because the walls were thin, and the lighting in the kitchen was terrible. And outside wasn't working any better.

She stood in the alley and guzzled the root beer, a Reitmann's Old Style. It opened with a strong sizzle on the gums, continuing with a cinnamon presence, and faded with a subtle vanilla flavor. Not bad, she judged. Three and a half out of five bubbles on the Mott and Amanda Bubble Scale.

Draining the bottle, she dropped it into the blue recycle

bin. And that's when she heard something go "mweep."

After the mweep came the distinct sound of nails scrabbling against cardboard.

Something was alive in there.

Probably a rat.

Mott didn't have anything against rats. Elmer was a rat. He'd lived in a roomy cage in Mott's fifth-grade class back in Pennsylvania, and he was friendly and clean, the kind of rat you could feed a carrot to and he wouldn't bite and give you a disease. Good old Elmer. Los Angeles garbage rats were probably entirely different. They were probably bitey.

Well, if a rat had gotten into the recycling on its own, it could get itself out.

Unless it couldn't.

Unless it was too small.

Or it was hurt.

"Mweep."

Mott tiptoed as close to the bin as she dared and stretched to peer inside. A flash of white fur appeared beneath a shifting piece of cardboard. Not a rat.

Mott looked up and down the alley in hopes of finding someone else to deal with this. Maybe an adult. Maybe another kid who looked like an animal lover or was practiced in the art of rodent combat.

But there was only her.

Holding her breath, she flicked the piece of cardboard aside and gasped.

Sitting amid discarded cans and bottles and boxes was a ball of white fluff with big triangular ears and a moist button nose. It blinked at her with eyes as blue as the ocean on a world map.

"Puppy!" Mott squeaked.

"Mweep," the puppy squeaked back.

Without another thought, Mott reached into the bin, lifted the puppy with both hands, and nuzzled him to her chest.

His fur was so soft, like petting air. Clean scents of pine and mountain snow wafted into Mott's nose. Since he didn't stink, he couldn't have been in the bin very long. And he was too small to have climbed in on his own, which meant someone had thrown him away as if he were garbage.

Anger rose like lava from Mott's belly and boiled in her head. Who would do such a thing to a tiny animal?

A massive, awful, disgusting jerk, that's who.

But did the puppy belong to the jerk? Maybe someone had dognapped him and then decided they didn't want him after all. Or maybe he was a stray. He had no collar, no tags.

"What do you think I should do?" Mott asked the pup.

He gave her a very serious look. "Mweep."

Mott stared into his blue eyes, and he stared back, and she knew what he wanted, and she knew what he needed.

"I promise—" Mott started to say, but stopped.

A promise was more than words that spilled from your lips. A promise was an action. And when you broke a promise, you broke a lot of things. You broke a trust. You could break a heart. She knew this because people she trusted had promised her things and then broken those promises.

She thought it over.

Then, knowing the full weight of her next words, she completed them. "I promise I'm going to take care of you."

"Mweep," said the pup.

"You are one hundred percent correct: Whoever threw you in the recycling is gross. And I know you don't speak English and I don't speak pup, but I'm going to pretend we're both having a conversation, because otherwise I'm just talking to myself, and talking to you is better. Okay?"

The pup was too busy sniffing the air with his twitching nose to answer.

There was an animal shelter less than a mile walk down

Overland Avenue, a squat brick building that announced its presence from blocks away with a chorus of barks and yips.

By the time Mott arrived on foot, huge love for the pup had bloomed in her heart. It wasn't a completely welcome feeling. Especially not here at the shelter.

A week after arriving in Culver City, even before they'd unpacked all their belongings, her mom had taken her here to look at dogs. It was supposed to be compensation for having to move from Pennsylvania, to give her something to look forward to. To give her a friend. Mott had quickly fallen in love with a Chihuahua/terrier/Lab mix named Benson, and they put in an application, and it even got approved.

But then her mom's new company had cutbacks, and her job disappeared. The rent on the nice, new apartment was too much, and they ended up moving again, to a smaller, less nice apartment. It would have been okay. Mott would have adjusted her expectations. She'd done it before. But this apartment had a no-dogs policy.

"Mweep," said the pup with outrage.

Mott steeled herself and walked through the door.

Inside, a handful of people clacked on computers or talked on phones. The barking was even louder, and despite a lemony tinge of cleaning products, the place smelled strongly of dog. The pup shifted in Mott's arms and fluttered with a growl. It was a very cute growl.

"Who's this?" said the person at the desk, using the high-pitched voice people use when talking to small baby animals. He had silver-gray hair and big forearms and wore a powder blue polo shirt with the animal shelter name printed over the pocket.

"I don't know. I found him in a recycling bin. Someone threw him away."

The shelter guy didn't seem shocked, just disappointed. Then he gave Mott a look of recognition.

"Weren't you here before with your mom? You were going to adopt—"

"Benson."

He made a sympathetic noise. "I'm sorry that didn't work out. I know that must have been a gut punch." Mott fought down a lump in her throat. Her eyes felt hot. "Benson found a good forever family," he said. "I don't know if that makes you feel better or worse."

It made Mott feel both ways at the same time. She cleared her throat.

Shelter Guy scratched the dog's chin. "No tags, huh?"

"No. But I figured he might have a microchip."

"That was good thinking. Come on back."

Shelter Guy led Mott into an office. Framed quotes by people Mott assumed were famous hung on the walls:

Some people talk to animals. Not many listen, though. That's the problem. —A. A. Milne

Clearly, animals know more than we think, and think a great deal more than we know. —Irene M. Pepperberg

Outside of a dog, a book is man's best friend. Inside of a dog, it's too dark to read. —Groucho Marx

The shelter guy took a close look at pup's eyes and ears and teeth. The pup didn't seem to mind.

"Are you a veterinarian?" Mott asked.

"No, just a volunteer animal lover. Like you." As he kept examining the pup, a frown formed on his face.

"What's wrong?"

"He seems in good health," he said. "It's just . . ." The frown remained.

He got out an electronic device.

Mott put a protective hand on the pup's back. "Will it hurt?"

Shelter Guy shook his head. "Not a bit. Microchips are tiny, like grains of rice. If he's got one, the scanner will show me a code, and then I can look it up on the computer and it'll tell me who owns him."

"Okay, then. You can go ahead."

"Thank you very much."

"Oh, wait. I can't pay you. I don't have any money. I spent it on root beer."

"I hope it was a good root beer."

"Reitmann's," Mott volunteered. "It was pretty good. Three and a half bubbles."

Shelter Guy ran the scanner over the pup's front shoulders. Then under his front legs. Then down his back. Then over his hind legs and shoulders.

The scanner didn't beep or buzz. It made no noise at all.

"Well?" Mott asked.

"No microchip, I'm afraid."

Mott discovered she was actually happy about this. Maybe she didn't have to hand the pup over. At least not right away.

"You found him in the recycling bin, you said?"

"Behind Mi-T-Mart. I was recycling my root beer bottle.

"Please don't eat my hand, little scruff." The pup was trying to get Shelter Guy's entire hand in his jaws.

"Do you know what kind of dog he is?" Mott asked.

Shelter Guy's frown dug even deeper. "Kid, this isn't a dog. This is a wolf."

A WOLF.

The pup was a wolf.

Mott had found a wolf. She'd *rescued* a wolf.

She could be a girl with a wolf, like some kind of cool fantasy character. Maybe she'd get a sword. Maybe she'd start a new video channel. Really, she didn't know what she should do, but being a girl with a wolf was definitely going to be her thing. It was even better than root beer.

"You did good, kid," the shelter guy said while the pup . . . the wolf . . . glared suspiciously at its own tail as if it had just discovered it.

"What should I feed him?" Mott asked. "Meat, right? I think we have some hamburger in the freezer at home."

"He should be getting regurgitated meat and mother's milk. Regurgitated means—"

"Barfed up. Ew. I bet they don't sell meat barf in pet stores. Well, maybe I could get some moose or elk or deer at the supermarket and blend it up. . . ."

She imagined playing fetch with him in the park. Watching TV on the sofa with him curled up in her lap. Maybe at the end of summer when school began again, she could take him to class for show-and-tell. She wouldn't be the new girl. She'd be the girl with the wolf. It would be awesome, a ten-out-of-five-bubbles situation. If nothing else, the wolf would be her friend.

And then reality crashed down on her like a dinosaur-killing asteroid.

"I can't keep him."

"No. I'm sorry."

"He needs some kind of wolf-rescue organization," she said. "So they can release him into the wild."

Shelter Guy's face became very kind. "A lot of people would have just left him in that bin, but you brought him to us, and now we can make sure he goes to people who know how to take care of him."

With his tail in his mouth, the wolf made muffled growls.

"Will I be able to visit him?"

"I wouldn't get my hopes up. The best thing for him is to be rehabilitated and released into the wild with a pack of his own. He needs to roam and hunt as far away from people as possible. He needs freedom."

"Yeah," Mott said, so quietly she could barely hear her own voice. "Okay."

"I know a good organization," he tried to reassure her. "They're in Idaho. It's really pretty up there."

Mott believed him that the organization was good. She believed him that it was pretty. She believed him that it was best for the puppy. She also believed her heart was breaking.

With the matter apparently settled, Shelter Guy nodded. "I want to check him over a bit more. Would you like to help?"

"Okay," Mott repeated desperately. If she had to say goodbye to the pup, she wanted to spend every last second with him she could.

"Let's just get a leash on and walk him around to see how he moves." He produced a leash from a drawer and approached the pup with the looped end.

The pup's eyes narrowed. He flattened his ears against his head, and his tail shot out in straight and rigid line.

His snarl was tiny, but his teeth looked like needles. With shocking speed, he leaped to the floor and shot out of the room.

"Puppy, stop!" Mott cried, following the pup down the short corridor to the lobby.

Another shelter worker sprung from behind her desk to block the pup's path, but he easily darted around her.

"Look, everyone calm down," Shelter Guy said. "You're just freaking him out." He still held the leash.

The pup didn't slow down. Instead, he aimed himself straight for the exit.

Mott winced when he smashed headfirst into the glass door, which shattered in a gut-clenching crunch, blasting apart with hundreds of glittering square bits that clattered to the floor.

The pup kept going, out onto the sidewalk and away.

"Careful!" Shelter Guy warned. "Don't cut yourself."

Mott didn't care about cutting herself. She only cared about the pup. What if he was hurt? What if he ran into traffic? What if she'd already broken her promise to take care of him?

Outside, he was nowhere in sight. How could he have gotten lost so fast? How had such a small animal been strong enough to break through the glass?

Shelter Guy joined Mott on the sidewalk. "Which way did he go?"

"I don't know. I'll go right; you go left."

He handed her the leash. "If you find him, bring him back here, understand? He's not a pet."

Mott took the leash and started her search with a bitter taste in her mouth. She wasn't the one who'd sent him into a panic by trying to leash him, so why was she the one getting lectured?

"Puppy?" she called. She checked around trees and under bushes. She peered beneath parked cars and even stopped to look in a couple of garbage cans and recycling bins, anywhere the pup might be hiding. "Fuzz ball? Little wolf?"

She reached the end of the block and heard a faint "Mweep?"

Around the corner she went, sprinting.

There was the pup, alive, with no blood or other marks on him.

He was not alone.

Held off the ground, he wriggled and squirmed between a pair of massive hands belonging to a gigantic man wearing a brown jacket sewn with leather cords as thick as Mott's shoelaces and lined with animal fur. His pants were the same, tucked into fur boots. Brown hair tumbled over his broad shoulders, and a bushy beard fell over his chest.

He looked like a bear wearing another bear.

It must have been a costume. There were two movie studios in Culver City less than a mile from here, and the coffee shops were always full of studio workers and sometimes background actors. He was probably just an extra.

But he looked like he could flatten Mott like a bug.

"Put him down," Mott said. "He doesn't like the way you're squeezing him."

"I cannot." The man's voice was gentler than Mott expected. "He is too good at escaping."

"Are you the one who put him in the recycling?"

"What is recycling?"

"The garbage? Behind Mi-T-Mart? Did you throw him in the garbage?"

The man shook his head. "No. That sounds cruel. I am Gorm the Vicious, not Gorm the Cruel. Now please, small girl, step out of my way."

Mott planted her feet firmly on the sidewalk. "I said put him down."

16

He smiled under his beard. "You are brave. Or stupid. Sometimes it's hard to tell the difference. But I am Tew's bondsman, and my chieftain has given me a task."

"Who's Tew?"

Gorm gave her a look like she'd just asked what a shoe was. "If you don't know already, you don't want to. And now, brave one, you are wasting my time. This is your last warning. Move."

Mott gulped. "I have a task, too. I'm taking care of this pup."

"A pup?" He laughed, but not the kind of laugh people do when they think something's funny. "He is not a pup."

"I know. He's a wolf."

"Fenris is no ordinary wolf. He is the moon-eater. The Odin-slayer. The world-ender. He may be small on the outside, but his capacity for destruction is vast."

"Are you from one of the studios?" Mott asked. "I mean, your dialogue. It's . . . a lot."

Gorm's eyebrows knotted in a frown. He took a step toward her. She'd made him mad. He seemed like the wrong kind of person to make mad.

A burst of movement and a flap of feathers drew Mott's attention to the top of a palm tree. Two large crows took flight with shrill caws that stabbed the inside of Mott's head. On reflex, she closed her eyes and covered her ears, just for an instant. When she opened her eyes again, the crows were gone.

So was Gorm the Vicious.

Vanished.

Nowhere in sight.

The pup sat on the sidewalk, thumping his little tail.

"Weird," Mott said.

"Mweep," agreed the pup.

Mott knelt and scritched him behind his ears.

The pup gazed at her with his startling blue eyes and released a mighty belch.

Mott called the shelter and got transferred to Shelter Guy. "I found him," she said. "He's fine. No blood, no cuts, no glass between his toes."

Shelter Guy sounded relieved and told her to bring him back, but Mott told him no way. "You freaked him out with a leash and made him dive through a glass door. He could have got hit by a car or run off and hid forever. He's safer with me than with you."

Shelter Guy had a lot of things to say, but Mott didn't

hear them because she hung up while he was in midsentence.

But Mott wasn't going to lie to herself. She knew she couldn't keep Fenris. She'd just hold on to him until the wolf rescue organization got sorted out. Then she'd let him go. She'd promised to take care of him, and she would, even if it broke her heart.

Now it was time for some math.

Pup who's actually a baby wolf. Plus baby wolf who can dive through a glass door without a scratch. Plus big beardy guy claiming the baby wolf is actually a moon-eating monster.

It added up to a kind of weirdness that Mott couldn't ignore. She needed answers. So she went to the library.

Normally Mott would have walked right up to the reference desk and told the librarian what she was looking for, but the contraband wolf complicated things. She clutched him to her belly and hunched over as if she had a stomachache and headed for the encyclopedias.

The beardy guy had called the wolf Fenris.

She found an entry for "Fenris" and whispered a summary for the pup. "Your name is from Norse mythology, stuff believed by the ancient Vikings and their even more ancient ancestors. They didn't write things down, so their myths were recorded hundreds of years later. I bet that means they got some stuff wrong."

"Mweep," agreed Fenris.

She read the whole entry.

"Little pup, this is not good," she whispered when she got to the end. There was a drawing of a full-grown Fenris, red-eyed, bristly-haired, teeth like spikes. He was rearing up on his hind legs, grasping the moon with his front paws, ripping valleys into the lunar surface, about to snap down his jaws.

The caption read, "Fenris eats the moon during Ragnarok."

Fenris mweeped.

Mott fetched the "R" volume of the encyclopedia and snuck off between the bookshelves. Putting Fenris down, she sat on the carpet and began to read.

Ragnarok was a prophecy that foretold the end of the worlds.

Apparently, there was more than one world. Maybe they were talking about Mars and Jupiter and the rest.

She wrote "Ragnarok" in her root beer journal and started a list:

- Three winters, each longer than the last, with no summer between.
- Men forget the bonds of kinship.
- The golden rooster crows to summon the gods.
- The rust-red rooster crows to raise the dead in Helheim.
- The Ship of Dead Men's Nails delivers the dead back to the lands of the living.
- The Midgard serpent, venom-spitting, raises the seas.
- Surtur, flame-wielding, sets the land on fire.
- The wolf Fenris swallows the moon and sun.
- An age of axes. An age of swords. And an age of wolves, till the world goes down.

She laid her palm on Fenris's side and watched it rise and fall. She took a sniff of his clean fur. She cooed at his tiny pink toe beans.

Moon-eater, the beardy man had called him.

World-ender.

Also, chickens were involved.

"This is all pretty far-fetched," she said to Fenris. "Maybe you're just small but strong enough to break glass."

Curled at her feet, Fenris snoozed.

"No dogs allowed," announced a harsh voice, like the sound of doom. But it was just a teenager pushing a library cart.

Mott gathered up Fenris and reshelved the encyclopedia. The pup wasn't a myth. He was warm. When he sniffed, his nose vibrated. When she looked at him, he looked back, and she felt they saw each other. He was very real. But she couldn't escape the feeling that he was somehow even more than that.

She didn't know what to believe, but she'd promised to take care of the pup, so she took him home.

3

STEAM BILLOWED FROM A KETTLE on the stove top, filling the apartment with smells of garlic and spices and sweet soy sauce. Mott's mom was home.

"You're here," Mott said, trying not to sound like she was hiding a small and possibly mythically destructive wolf cub against her belly beneath her T-shirt.

"Yeah, Sonia at the restaurant had a doctor's appointment, so I agreed to trade shifts, which means I have to work tonight—sorry—but that gave me the afternoon free, so I figured I'd make you an early dinner—I hope bami goreng is okay—but then I have to catch the ten bus and transfer to the two to get to the museum. . . ."

Mott tried to keep the pup quiet while her mom stirred

the pot and rattled off the dizzying details of work sched-
ules and bus routes.

It wasn't supposed to be like this. For the first time since
she and Dad had split up, Mom was supposed have one job
that paid her enough to buy a car and afford rent on a nice
apartment with a big swimming pool and basketball courts
and a koi pond. One that allowed dogs.

Lots of broken promises.

"Oh, I got you a root beer at the store," her mom said,
reaching into the fridge. "It's a Burpenschlitt. Have you
reviewed that one yet?"

Mott was happy to talk about root beer all night long
if it distracted her mom from the drooling fuzz Mott was
carrying.

Her mom turned around with the root beer bottle in
her outstretched arm.

"Burpenschlitt, yes!" Mott said, too enthusiastically.
"Strong carbonation, leaves a pleasant ginger aftertaste on
the tongue. Four bubbles out of five."

Her mom's eyes narrowed. "Mott. Why do you have a
puppy?"

For one frantic moment, Mott considered claiming that
the canine-shaped animal she was carrying was, in fact, a

rare and very large breed of hamster. She even got so far into this plan that she decided to name this made-up breed a wolf hamster.

It might have worked, too, if only her mom didn't have more brains than a potted fern.

So Mott explained. She started with the discovery in the recycling bin behind Mi-T-Mart. She praised herself for taking the pup to the shelter. She performed a dramatic interpretation of the pup's reaction to the leash and an even more dramatic demonstration of his escape through the glass of the shelter's door.

But she left out one big part: Gorm the Vicious, the guy in the leathers and furs. Because technically, legally, Mott should have had adult supervision during the day, but it was summer and school wasn't in session, and the summer school and parks-and-rec programs were all full, and since Mott and her mom were new in town, they didn't know anybody who could take care of Mott when her mom was at work—not that Mott felt she needed anyone to take care of her, but if her mom knew about people like Gorm, Mott would be spending the summer indoors, gazing wistfully out the window.

Mott also left out the bit about Fenris possibly being

a world-ending monster.

Her mom put a hand on Mott's shoulder when she was done talking. "You, daughter, are a good person."

"Mweep," agreed the pup.

"But you know we can't keep him, right? The apartment policy . . ."

"I know," Mott said dismally.

She put the pup on the floor, and her mom crouched down to pet him. "So first thing tomorrow morning, we have to . . . OH MY GOD HE IS SO SOFT!" Fenris wiggled happily as she scritched his belly. "HOW IS HE SO SOFT?"

"Mweep," explained the pup.

Her mom's face scrunched up. "OH NO THAT WAS A VERY CUTE SOUND." She went back to scritching him.

Maybe there was hope. If her mom was as smitten with the pup as Mott was, if she fell in love and couldn't bear the thought of giving him away, and if the apartment manager also fell in love and tore up the no-dogs policy . . .

"Did the shelter say what kind of dog he is?" her mom asked. "He looks like a husky to me. Or maybe Alaskan malamute?"

"Um," Mott said. "Actually, turns out he's a wolf."

Fenris booped Mom's finger.

"We can't keep him," she said.

Shelter Guy came over with some formula and a little bit of pureed organic lamb and talked to Mott's mom. They agreed that Mott could keep the pup until the wolf rescue organization came the day after tomorrow to take the pup away forever. But under no circumstances, he declared, would Mott be keeping the wolf longer than that, and Mott's mom was in agreement on that as well.

So after Mott's mom left for a night shift at the diner, Mott made up her mind to enjoy the remaining time she had with the wolf. They played chase for a full hour, bouncing off the furniture, rolling around on the floor. There was a lot of wrestling and giggling and mweeping. By the time the pup finally ran out of gas, Mott was exhausted.

"Had enough?"

The pup's eyelids grew heavy. He turned in a circle a few times on the blanket Mott laid down next to her bed.

She sat on the floor with him and showed him pictures on her phone.

"This is our old apartment in Pennsylvania. That's

where I lived until a few weeks ago. It was bigger than this one, but they also had a no-dogs policy. I thought of getting a hamster or a rat, but I'm not a rodent kind of girl. I know some people like them, so I'm not judging."

Mott scrolled through more pictures.

She paused at one that gave her a flat, lukewarm sadness.

It was a selfie from this past January of her and her dad, the last time she'd seen him, when he'd taken her to North Bowl in Philadelphia for pinball and pizza. There was a half-eaten medium pepperoni-and-spinach pie on the table, two plastic tumblers of root beer, dad's cup still full, Mott's almost empty. Mott remembered the crash of bowling pins filling the silences between them. She hadn't minded the silences. Silence contained no lies.

"How's the root beer?"

"A strong four of five."

The root beer was some big mass-produced brand and tasted like corn syrup, worth maybe two bubbles at the most, but Mott was scoring it a four, because lunches with Dad were rare, and the rareness gave the root beer extra value.

"Okay," Dad said. "So let's talk about your late Christmas present."

"It's okay, Dad, you don't have to—"

"You don't want a video camera?"

"I mean, yeah, but—"

"You don't want studio lights?"

"That would be totally—"

"And you're still using your mom's old laptop? If you're going to keep doing the root beer thing, you're going to need a machine that's up to the task, right?"

Mott didn't really need any of those things. She just needed more times like this with Dad, whether it was pizza places or bowling alleys or just driving somewhere in the car. She just needed *him*.

Not that new video recording gear wouldn't be amazing.

"Yeah," he said, as if they'd just settled the matter. "We're going to get you set up."

And then he ruined everything by saying the cursed words: "I promise." And Mott knew it was all just talk.

The puppy scooched closer to Mott, as if he could tell she was lost in a sad memory, and Mott gently scritched him behind the ear.

He stretched his jaws in a yawn.

A strange sensation overtook Mott. The world was

spinning. Or she was. She felt herself pitching forward toward the pup's yawning mouth.

When Mott and her mom moved west in their rented truck packed with everything they owned, they took a detour to see the Grand Canyon, because if they were going to drive across the country, her mom figured they should actually see the country. Mott remembered standing on a U-shaped observation deck, nothing but a thin pane of glass between her shoes and the bottom of the deep chasm hundreds of feet below. But it wasn't fear of falling that had made her dizzy, that had made her feel she was outside her own body. It was the canyon's sheer size. It was too wide. Too far across. Too deep. Too massive. It was too much to take in all at once, like the sight of it was hitting her eyes and her brain didn't know what to do with all that information.

The puppy's yawning mouth made her feel the same way.

It was broader than it should have been.

Vast.

Bottomless.

Empty.

The pup closed his mouth and the feeling faded. He curled up, and after a few minutes, he peacefully snored.

"I'm just dehydrated," Mott decided. "That's all."

She fetched a Reitmann's Old Style from the fridge and returned to her room. After popping open the bottle, she took a sip, let the root beer sit on her tongue before swallowing. She still wanted to post a video, so she got out her phone and recorded a review and posted it to the channel before she lost her nerve.

The comments started coming in fast.

"Was this filmed in a cave? Get some lights!"

"Where's the other girl?"

"I miss Amanda. Where's Amanda???"

"I miss her, too, you mean bozo," she said, deleting the video.

She texted Amanda, even though Amanda probably wouldn't see it for a long time. They always supported each other when they got mean comments.

She watched the pup sleep. His paws flicked and he made tiny squeaks as he chased rabbits or birds in his dreams, just like any puppy would.

But he was not a dog, Mott reminded herself. He was a wolf. A wolf capable of smashing through a glass door without suffering a scratch. A wolf that had been held captive by a huge, strangely dressed man who completely vanished when Mott turned her head. A wolf that yawned and made Mott feel like she was falling into a black hole.

"Can you really be *that* Fenris?" she whispered.

The pup let out a tiny snore.

THE PUP BOUNDED IN THE damp grass, chasing butterflies and growling at dandelions. Mott hadn't wanted to spend her remaining time with the pup moping inside and waiting for the wolf rescue organization to call, so she'd taken him to the park.

The sky was covered in a gray blanket that kept in the heat, and the air felt like soup. Los Angeles was supposed to have perfect weather, but Mott was convinced the place was just one continuing natural disaster. In the last week alone she'd seen torrential rain and blasting heat. There'd been brushfires in the Hollywood Hills, and she'd heard about fancy homes in Malibu sliding into the sea. She hadn't experienced an earthquake yet, but at least that was something to look forward to.

She sat crisscross applesauce while the pup ran circles around her. "You're going to like the wolf rescue," she assured him. "You'll get all the regurgitated meat you want, and when you get bigger, I bet they'll let you hunt an entire buffalo. I don't know if they have buffalo in Idaho, so please don't consider that a promise. But you'll have plenty of space to roam and a whole pack of buddies. I bet you'll howl at the moon and . . . it'll be great."

Unless he was a moon-eating monster.

She felt silly just thinking about it.

The pup quit bothering butterflies and flowers and curled up in Mott's lap. Mott scritched his snoot, and he licked her hand. Every time he did something cute like this, the cracks in Mott's heart deepened.

"I don't want this to be a sad day," she declared. "I want to enjoy this."

"Mweep," Fenris said with hearty approval.

They walked to the ice cream shop in the strip mall half a mile from home, welcoming the chilled air when they went in.

"Hey, no dogs," drawled the guy behind the counter. He was standing with a scooper in his hands but looked as though he'd just woken from a nap.

"He's not a dog. He's a wolf."

The scoop guy blinked lazily. "Whoa, gnarly. So what do you want?"

Mott studied the menu board. "Is there such a thing as wolf-safe ice cream?"

"Dunno, I'm not a zoolologist."

"I think you put an extra 'lol' in there."

"No, I didn't."

People who were sure they were right when they were actually wrong weren't Mott's favorite people, but since he wasn't kicking Mott and the pup out, Mott decided not to argue.

"How much is a large root beer float with vanilla ice cream?"

He told her the price.

Mott counted all her money. She'd earned her root beer fund by doing laundry for some of the old folks in the Pennsylvania apartment, but it was already running low.

The door jingled, and in walked a reedy old man in a moth-eaten sweater.

Fenris squirmed in Mott's arms.

"Hey, I thought I told you," the guy with the scooper said, "no free ice cream."

The old man gasped, offended. "But why not?"

"Because we live in a society, and there are rules, and the number one rule is you have to pay for ice cream."

Mott got the feeling that this wasn't the first time they'd had this conversation.

The man gave the ice cream guy a keen look with one clear gray eye. His other eye was either missing or hidden in a squint.

"And what of the older rules?" he said in a quavering voice. "What about the rules of kindness? What about the rules of hospitality?"

"I'm being hospitable by not tossing your butt out of here."

"That's mean," Mott said.

"Yeah, but—" the ice cream buy began, but Mott cut him off.

"There's never an excuse to be mean."

"Yeah, but—" the ice cream guy tried again.

"I'd be happy to buy you a scoop," she said to the old man.

He turned his gaze on her. "This is what I'm talking about. Hospitality. Kindness. You have a good heart." There was a sternness about him, despite his frailty. A seriousness.

Fenris whimpered.

"Thank you," was all Mott could think to say.

"I would like a single scoop on a sugar cone, please," he said to the ice cream guy. "Root beer flavored."

"I didn't know they had root beer ice cream."

"Indeed. It's the finest of their thirty-two flavors. I recommend it."

Grumbling, the ice cream guy scooped the old man's order and handed him the cone. The old man held it aloft as if it were some sacred object. He turned back to Mott. "May you be ever favored," he said. Then he regarded Fenris with a deep squint. "Heh, puppy."

And with that, he was out the door.

Mott counted her money again. She no longer had enough for a float, so she settled on a scoop. "I'll take what he had."

A few minutes later, she and the pup sat on a grass island in the parking lot. Fenris seemed nervous, hunching over and letting out soft whimpers.

"Hey, what's wrong?"

He gave her a pitiful look.

"You want some ice cream?"

His look turned hopeful.

"Okay, but just the teeniest taste. I don't want to get you sick."

She dipped a fingertip into her scoop and let the pup lick a tiny dab.

"Mweep!"

"Good stuff, right?"

Mott imagined what her life could be with the pup. Lazy summer days in the park. Eating ice cream floats with her little buddy. Sneaking him into movie theaters. Maybe putting him in a little sweater. Or a big sweater, because it probably wouldn't take long until he outweighed her and she'd be trying to find him elk to eat.

Today was only for today, she remembered.

"Well, pup, at least we have this."

"Are you out of your mind?" boomed a voice.

A girl took long strides across the parking lot toward Mott. She had a broad pale face with rosy cheeks, framed by a pair of copper-blond braids. She wore a white wool pullover shirt embroidered with red squiggles beneath a leather vest trimmed with fur. Her baggy red pants were tucked into worn black leather boots. Slung over her shoulder was a leather duffel bag, and the thing sticking out of it was most definitely the handle of a sword.

"That wolf is dangerous."

The puppy blepped his tongue and made an awkward puppy lunge at the girl.

Mott scooped him up in her arms and rose to her feet. "How do you know he's a wolf? You're not with the wolf rescue."

"I am the *you* rescue," declared the girl. "I am rescuing you from the wolf."

"I don't need a rescue. He's not going to hurt anyone, are you, fuzz?" Mott tickled him under the chin.

"Mweep." The puppy squirmed in her arms.

"You don't know what you're dealing with. I am Thrudi, and he is my prisoner."

Mott swallowed. The girl, Thrudi, was another one of those people, like Gorm the Vicious, and this time Mott couldn't pretend they were extras from a movie set.

But that didn't mean Fenris was a monster. It didn't mean he would eat the moon. It didn't mean the world was ending.

"Are you the one who put him in the recycling bin? Because if you did . . ."

"What is recycling?"

"Recycling . . . it's like garbage, but better. How do you

not know what recycling is?"

Thrudi grunted. "This is not my world. Neither is it Fenris's. Unhand him."

She wasn't much bigger than Mott, but her glare could have burned holes in concrete. Mott got the feeling that if she wanted to, the girl could beat her like an egg.

"You can't have him."

Thrudi smiled. It was not a friendly smile. "You don't know what you're dealing with. You think he's a gentle cub, an infant. But he is older and more dangerous than you can imagine. He is the Odin-slayer. The son of Loki. Fenris, god-foe. Fenris, moon-eater. Fenris, ender of worlds."

Mott winced. Even if she didn't believe Fenris was a world-killer, the girl obviously did. "Why do you people talk so weird?"

"We don't talk weird."

"Yeah, you do. You're all 'Lo and forsooth, beware the puppy, for he will, like, wreak havoc upon all you know.'"

"Well, you people are all 'I have a bank account. Those shoes are cool. Have you seen my trombone?'"

"I literally have never said any of those things."

"Well, that's what I've been told," the girl said stubbornly.

"Whatever. Come on, fuzz, we're leaving." Mott started walking away. Behind her, she heard a *shruff*. She turned back around. Held in Thrudi's hand, a long object gleamed in the sun.

"Why do you have a sword?"

Thrudi opened her mouth, but before she got a word out, the pup sprang from Mott's arms. Like a fuzzy cannonball, he raced to the girl and leaped for her chest. She windmilled her arms to keep her balance but fell back onto the asphalt, her sword clanging on the ground.

Mott rushed to pick it up. She raised it with both hands. "You'd better not hurt him."

Thrudi didn't pay Mott any attention. She was too busy trying to defend herself against the pup.

"Stop it, beast! I wasn't going to hurt her. No, don't! Wolf spit, gah! So gross!"

Actually, it wasn't much of an attack. The pup was licking her face. His tail wagged in a happy blur.

Mott watched for a while, both amused and confused. She felt self-conscious holding the sword.

The pup grew tired and soon was snoring with his snout buried in Thrudi's armpit. "Very well," Thrudi muttered, stroking his back. The pup continued to sleep.

Mott suffered a pang of jealousy.

"He belongs to you?"

"As I said, I'm his guard. But he escaped his prison, and I've been in pursuit this past day. Gladly, I tracked him here instead of a more dangerous world."

"If you're Fenris's guard, that means you're responsible for him ending up in the recycling bin. And I promised Fenris I'd take care of him, so he's staying with me."

Thrudi nodded. "You gave an oath. That is admirable. I respect it. Unless you break your oath. Where I come from, 'oath-breaker' is among the vilest insults. It's right up there with troll-butt and bedpan-drinker."

"Ew," Mott said. And, "I'm not an oath-breaker."

"We shall see."

"There was a man yesterday," Mott said. "He was dressed like you."

"Did he give his name?"

"Gorm the Vicious. And he mentioned someone else. Tew."

Thrudi let out a breath through her nostrils. "This is bad. Tew is strife. He is anger and chaos and pain and death. Tew is a god of war."

"What does he want with Fenris?"

"They're enemies. The prophecy of Ragnarok says the worlds are thrown into chaos and devastation, and then Fenris eats the moon, and then Fenris eats Odin, and then Odin's son, Vidar, kills Fenris. The universe dies. Tew is looking forward to it. He would like to hasten events, and by wielding Fenris's destructive might as a weapon, he can ensure that the chaos and devastation happen."

"He's just a puppy," Mott said. "He can't destroy anything." Except, there was the window at the shelter. And the bottomless yawn. Mott had to be honest with herself. Was it that she didn't believe, or was it that she didn't want to? "Anyway," she said, "I promised to take care of him."

Something in Thrudi's attitude changed. "I made my own promise to take care of him. To stand guard over him. To keep him from doing harm. But I failed. Now I have to fix things. So, I ask you, girl—"

"My name is Martha. People call me Mott."

Thrudi rose to her feet. "Then I ask you, Mott. Will you surrender Fenris so I can keep him out of trouble?"

"Tomorrow morning he's getting picked up by a wolf rescue organization. They're going to take him all the way to Idaho."

"What is Idaho?"

"It's a place. Mountains. Trees. Squirrels. Other wolves. You know, nature stuff."

"And it's far?"

"Very far. Unimaginably, unfairly, painfully far."

Thrudi rubbed her chin. "Hmm. This Idaho sounds promising. Few of us Asgardians have been to Midgard in a very long time. Perhaps Idaho is a good solution. You said this . . . this rescue organization is taking him tomorrow?"

"Yes. And today, he and I are going to hang out. We're going to goof around and have fun. While we still can."

Thrudi widened the distance between her feet, ready to spring, like a martial arts stance. "I am not leaving the animal alone in your custody. That is final."

Mott didn't have a stance, but that didn't mean she was going to back down.

"Then you have two choices," she said, hoping her voice made her seriousness and determination clear. "You can leave us alone. Or you can join us for fun."

Thrudi let out a short, grim huff. "Very well," she said. "Let us have fun."

5

THRUDI RODE A PINK CAMEL. "Is this fun?"

"Fenris thinks it's fun." With Fenris in her lap, Mott rode a unicorn.

Secretly, she didn't think the carousel was exceptionally fun, with distorted music coming from battered speakers and the achingly slow progress of the animals as they creaked around and around. Also, her unicorn was kind of sticky.

"What do you do for fun?" she asked when the ride came to an end. Who knew what kind of lavish entertainment Thrudi was used to? Probably something better than a temporary carnival on the edge of a supermarket parking lot.

"Mostly we hurl sharp objects at one another."

"We can do that here," Mott said, cheered.

She led Thrudi to the midway and with the last of her money bought Thrudi a ticket at the dart-throwing booth.

Thrudi hefted three darts in her hand. "Who do I throw these at?"

"You don't throw them at anyone. You throw them at the balloons."

"And balloons are . . ."

"Those rubber things on the wall?"

The back wall of the booth was festooned with a few dozen under-inflated balloons against a white board pricked with holes. Every hole was a miss.

"And if I hit them, I get to keep the balloons?"

The booth operator pointed out the neon-colored stuffed animals on the shelf above. "Hit enough, and you win a prize."

"I see," said Thrudi. "Like this?"

Barely aiming, she released the darts.

Whoosh–whoosh–whoosh went the darts.

Pop–pop–pop went the balloons.

"This is no challenge," Thrudi said. "They don't even run. Are you sure there's nobody to throw them at?"

Five minutes later, Thrudi struggled along with a giant purple stuffed hippo. "That turned out to be very fun!"

"You really weren't supposed to just take the hippo like that."

"But when I hit the balloons the man went back on his word and refused to award me a prize."

"You were supposed to buy more darts."

"Then he should have said so. I cannot abide a trickster."

They walked on in silence. Every few steps, Mott glanced over her shoulder. So far they weren't being pursued by carnival workers or cops.

"I'm sorry," Thrudi said after a while. "I should learn to follow your rules while I am here."

"He should have explained things better. I should have too. I didn't realize what a rip-off those games are." She found herself laughing. "But, wow, you're really great at throwing sharp objects."

"The sharper, the better. It's a big part of Valkyrie training. Also, it relaxes me. But if I'm going to face challenges in your land, I must know it better."

"Well, what do you want to know?"

"For starters, I'd like a better sense of the landscape."

"I can help you with that."

Carrying Fenris so he couldn't run into traffic, she led Thrudi up Jefferson Boulevard, alongside the straw-colored hills that bordered Culver City. They climbed a narrow road that went to a Little League baseball field and stood on the edge of the bluff, overlooking Los Angeles. Freeways carved the city into sections, each little glimmering dot crawling over them a car or truck. Mott and her mom had hiked up here after they moved in, but that had been a much prettier day. Now the skyscrapers downtown were all but hidden behind a smudge of yellow-brown air. In the other direction, the ocean was dull gray, and Mott could barely make out the Hollywood sign through the smog.

Thrudi stood with her hands on her hips, studying the city. "I didn't realize things had gotten so bad on Midgard."

"What's Midgard?"

"That's what we call your world." Thrudi pointed at a tree on the edge of center field. Mott's mom had told her it was an ash.

"Think of the universe as a tree," Thrudi said. "Each world is a root, separate, yet connected to the others. We are now on the root called Midgard, the world of mortal humans." She pointed to another root. "There are nine realms, nine worlds, in all. Helheim, land of the dead. Muspelheim, land of flames. Jotunheim, where the giants dwell. I'm from Asgard, a world of gods and monsters. Perhaps you've heard their names, even on your world. Odin? Thor? Loki?"

Mott nodded.

"To you, they are memories, so long ago and faded that their remnants have been rewoven as myth. But where I come from, they are daily reality."

"Do you also know Zeus and Hercules?"

"In a sense. All gods are reflections of each other, even the ones worshipped on your world. But my point is, Ragnarok is happening everywhere, in all the realms. In Asgard, we've suffered the worst winters in memory, three in a row. And your world is even worse than I'd feared."

Mott thought back to her bullet list. "Three winters? Each longer than the last?"

"Yes," Thrudi said, surprised.

"With no summer between?"

"Yes, exactly as foretold."

"Hm." Mott got out her root beer journal. Reluctantly, she drew a checkmark by the first item: "Three winters, each longer than the last, with no summer between."

"Things are getting worse in all the nine worlds, Mott. And Fenris has a role in it. You want to protect the little wolf from harm. But I need to prevent the realms from turning to dust and ash." She looked uncertain. "I at least have to try."

"Is it possible? To save the worlds from Ragnarok?"

Thrudi took a long time before answering. "No. It's not. Ragnarok is a promise the universe made on the day it was born. All living creatures make the same promise: that just as we live, one day we must die. And the universe is no oath-breaker. Ragnarok is inevitable."

Mott knew what "inevitable" meant. It meant that something was going to happen no matter what you did. Like it was inevitable that her dad would disappoint her. Like it was inevitable that eventually Mott would have to say goodbye to Fenris.

But not until tomorrow.

Clouds hovered over the sea like a gray cliff. Waves even darker than the clouds churned and clawed at the sand high up the beach. The ocean looked swollen.

"The world-spanning serpent grows restless beneath the sea," said Thrudi, another echo of the Ragnarok prophecy.

"Maybe it's just a regular storm," Mott countered. "People say sea levels have been rising for a while."

"Or maybe the serpent's been thrashing for a while."

Fenris trotted along with Mott and Thrudi down the boardwalk, a wide concrete path running along the beach. Despite the cold and drizzle, the boardwalk still teemed with roller skaters, musicians with open guitar cases playing for pocket change, artists selling paintings and homemade jewelry on rolled-out rugs. The shops blasted hip-hop and reggae.

On a blanket, a man was playing checkers with a rust-red rooster. Mott gave it a suspicious eye and consulted her root beer journal, where she'd written "The rust-red rooster crows to raise the dead in Helheim."

The rooster's checkers opponent hopped a black checker over three red checkers, and the red rooster let out a cluck and a half-hearted cock-a-doodle. Mott put her journal back in her pocket. No way did that count as a Ragnarok portent.

"You've been here before?" Thrudi asked, taking in the sights.

"My mom and I came here the day after we moved. We had pizza slices. Then we bought towels with the California flag on them and sunbathed on the sand. The weather was really nice that day."

Now that Mott thought back on it, it was the last truly good day she remembered.

"I know what you mean," Thrudi said. "One time my sisters and I were walking along the fjord and came across a beached Jotun ox. We built a fire and fed on him for days until vultures ran us off."

"Right," Mott said. "That . . . sounds . . . well . . ." She stopped in front of another shop. Thrudi's interests sounded pretty gross, so maybe she'd enjoy the gross things Venice Beach had to offer.

"Wanna see a dead man's hand?"

Thrudi's eyes got bright. "Always!"

Professor Griswald's Museum of the Strange and Curious and Gift Emporium sat between a cheap T-shirt shop and a cheap sunglasses stand. The door jingled, and Mott and Thrudi entered a cramped space jammed with display cases. Everywhere Mott looked was something strange, weird, gross, or all three: a taxidermy sheep with two faces, a rabbit with deer antlers, something labeled "The Fiji Mermaid" that looked like a monkey with a fish tail grafted on.

Fenris mweeped in wonder. Or maybe hunger. It was getting harder to tell.

"Have you ever seen such a place?" asked Mott.

"Certainly," Thrudi said. "This is very similar to a dwarven hoard, only much smaller."

"Hmph," said Mott, disappointed. She'd wanted Thrudi to be impressed.

"Welcome!" A red-cheeked man emerged from a back room, waving a feather duster. A tangled white beard fringed his jaw. "And welcome, small wolf pup. I hope you're house-trained. I'm Professor Griswald, curator of this fine establishment, and it is my proud privilege to present this exhibition of the unusual and unexpected. We also carry a line of high-quality souvenir keychains. Feel free to look around, ask questions if you have 'em."

Mott liked Griswald. He'd taken in the sight of a wolf pup and an armed Valkyrie without even blinking. "I guess you've seen a lot of strange things," she said, casting her gaze around for the mummified hand.

"Why, I've dedicated my entire life to them. The wonder! The magic! The souvenir keychains on which I'm offering a buy-one-get-one-free sale!" He scratched his beard with a thoughtful frown. "But to tell you the

53

truth, the oddest thing I've ever seen has been outside my window."

Thrudi went to the window. "What do you mean?"

"The weather," Griswald exclaimed. "Yesterday the ocean was flat as a tortilla, but look at it now. I'm a sailor, and I know what a brewing tempest looks like. I've seen eight so-called 'once-in-a-lifetime' storms just in the past two years. There's plenty of strangeness wherever you look: floods, droughts, typhoons, hurricanes, blizzards, and heat waves."

"What do you think's causing it?" Mott asked.

"You are," he said. "And me, too. All of us, with our factories and power plants and cars and planes. We're heating up the world and messing up the weather, melting glaciers, warming oceans, all that stuff."

"It's Jormungandr," Thrudi insisted. "The world-spanning serpent thrashes beneath the waves, lifting the sea."

"Maybe we're using different words for the same thing," Griswald said.

"Do you still have the mummified hand?" Mott asked.

Griswald's cheeks lit up. "Oh, you're a repeat customer, good! I moved it over here by the window so the sunlight catches its unpleasantly withered flesh."

Mott and Thrudi followed Griswald to a covered glass cake stand labeled "Hand of Uncertain Origin." Under the cover sat a thing that looked like a tarantula made from a rawhide dog chew. But it was a hand. It had four fingers and a thumb and black fingernails and was definitely human.

"Mweep," said Fenris.

"This is one of the finest dead man's hands I've ever seen," said Thrudi.

Mott was about to ask how much experience Thrudi had with the body parts of the dead when one of the fingers twitched.

Griswald jumped back.

Fenris mweeped.

Thrudi struck a combat pose.

"Does it usually do that?" Mott asked.

"It usually just lies in the case, nice and quiet, like you'd want a dead man's hand to behave."

The hand moved again, more than a twitch this time. It stood on its fingertips and spider-crawled up the side of the glass dome.

"How can a dead man's hand be alive?" Mott asked. Nobody answered, but she didn't blame them. It was sort of a philosophical question.

The hand tapped on the dome with its index finger, *tink-tink*, as if testing the strength of the glass.

"Girls, enjoy your tour of the museum," Griswald said. "I'm hiding."

"What about wonder and magic?" Mott asked.

"Sometimes wonder and magic are awful." With that, he and his feather duster retreated to the back room.

Mott got out her notebook and put a question mark next to "The Ship of Dead Men's Nails delivers the dead back to the lands of the living."

Thrudi was watching over her shoulder. "Just a question mark?"

"I'm trying not to jump to conclusions."

"There's a living dead hand right before your eyes, Mott."

The hand waved at them.

"Fine, okay, I'm convinced." She couldn't think of a better explanation for a living dead hand than the dead rising due to an ancient prophecy about the end of world, so she replaced the question mark with a bold checkmark. And she figured she might as well put a check next to "The rust-red rooster crows to raise the dead in Helheim." Not wanting to believe something wasn't an excuse not to believe it. "The world is ending. And Fenris . . ." The pup licked his chops at the dead man's hand. "Fenris is *that* Fenris."

Saying the words brought a surprising sense of relief. Maybe it was better to face reality than keep trying to deny it, even if the reality was terrible.

The hand pushed the cake dome lid to the ground. Glass shattered, and the hand was free. It zigged. It zagged. It skittered between display cases. It darted around displays of keychains and knocked over a whole spinner-rack of postcards. Pausing for just a second, as if marshaling its determination, it charged the door. On impact, the door swung open, and the dead man's hand scuttled down the boardwalk.

Mweeping with excitement, Fenris took off after it.

"No, Fenris, no!" screamed Mott, chasing after.

The hand dodged the legs of skaters and runners and walkers on the boardwalk. It was hard to know because it didn't have a face or a voice, but Mott thought it was scared. And with Fenris right behind it, she couldn't blame it. There was a ferocity in Fenris's eyes Mott hadn't seen before.

The hand hitched a ride on the back of a skateboard

before leaping onto a jogger's shoulder.

"Eyaaaaaaaagh," said the jogger, which Mott considered an understatement.

One brave woman tried to whip the hand away with her beach towel, but the hand saw that as an opportunity and used the towel as a bridge up her arm and onto her face.

From there, it leaped from head to head.

All these actions were accompanied by much screaming, which Mott thought was the only normal part of this whole ordeal.

Swooping down from the sky, a seagull snatched the hand. Fenris snarled and leaped, rising shockingly high for a pup with stubby legs. The gull carried the hand briefly before releasing it, apparently finding it too strange to eat.

For a seagull, that said a lot.

"Get it off!" howled a roller-blader when the hand clung to the back of his neck.

Mott caught up to him and managed to pry it away, but it was remarkably strong for a withered dead thing, and it squirmed out of her grip.

"Unnnghh," said the skater. "Gaaaaaghh."

The boardwalk was now enflamed in full-on panic. Shouting. Running. People with phones taking pictures and video as the hand scrambled in and out of a busker's guitar case, sending coins and crumpled dollar bills flying. Fenris ran across jewelry displays on blankets, leaving a trail of scattered trinkets and slobber.

Mott and Thrudi almost caught up to it again when a bike went speeding by. The hand got tangled up in the spokes of the rear tire, and the bike and rider clattered to the ground. The hand flew, sailing through the air and landing on the boardwalk with a thump.

Right in front of Fenris, who pinned it to the ground with two paws.

Trapped, the hand thrashed.

Fenris's eyes gleamed.

Mott saw how this was going to end. It was inevitable.

"Fenris, don't," she ordered anyway. "Don't you do it. Don't you eat that hand."

"Mweep," said Fenris.

And then he ate that hand.

"I KNOW THE APARTMENT'S NOT very big—" Mott began.

"It is a handsome home, but Tew remains a threat to Fenris. Please tell me about your fortifications. How many warriors are garrisoned here? How long can you hold out against a siege?"

Mott wasn't sure how to answer. "The door lock is pretty good. And we have an intruder alarm." She keyed the number pad on the wall to activate the alarm. "If anyone tries to come in, the alarm goes off."

Thrudi nodded. "That is clever magic. Who does the alarm summon?"

"The apartment manager."

Trudi smiled fiercely. "Ah, a mighty soldier eager to

make battle? I suggest we summon them now and prepare for conflict."

"No, he's just a guy named Eddie. He has a little office in the parking garage."

"He's not mighty?"

"Not really. But he can spit far."

"I see." Thrudi's smile faded, and she returned to examining the door and walls and windows.

Mott emptied some pureed lamb meat into a salad bowl and topped it off with formula. This was the last time she'd get to feed Fenris dinner before the wolf rescue people came tomorrow morning. And then he'd be safe. And very far away.

"Do you want something to eat or drink?" she asked Thrudi, trying to perk herself up. "We have root beer, OJ, milk, water . . . ?"

Thrudi rose from her knees, where she'd been peering judgmentally at the keyhole. "I do not know what root beer is, but it sounds interesting."

Mott popped open a bottle of Raging Bear with her pocketknife bottle opener and poured it into two chilled glasses from the back of the fridge.

Thrudi took a sip and her eyes went wide. She downed the rest without taking a breath. "This is delicious," she declared after an excellent burp.

"I know! Are you catching the subtle cinnamon bite and the chocolate aftertaste?"

"What is chocolate?"

"You don't know what chocolate is?"

"No, we don't have such a thing in Asgard."

"This is important: let's get some chocolate in you right now."

"First, I shall pee."

Thrudi was weird. Awesomely weird.

Mott showed her the bathroom and went back to check on Fenris in the kitchen. He was trying to clean a little bit of lamb stuck to his nose by smooshing his face against the floor. Then he noticed his own tail, growled at it, and presented his belly to Mott. Mott dutifully scritched him.

"It's hard to imagine you eating the moon and ending the world. You're so tiny and silly."

Thrudi came out of the bathroom, her hands looking pink and freshly scrubbed like a normal person's.

"My mom will be coming home soon," Mott said. "We'll need to come up with a story to explain you."

"There's nothing to explain. I'll hide in a bush and guard your home from the outside."

"That's ridiculous."

"I assure you, I'm used to rustic accommodations. Heh, reminds me of the time I slept inside a dead elk."

"Oh, my god."

"It wasn't bad at all. The elk was freshly killed."

"You're not sleeping in a dead elk, Thrudi."

Thrudi seemed confused by Mott's concern. "I'll be fine. This way I'll be able to spot any trouble early. If something happens, I'll call out for you and you can press the alarm to summon Eddie the Spitter."

Mott tried to convince Thrudi that sleeping in the bushes was silly and unnecessary and that it made Mott feel like a bad friend, even though they weren't friends. But she couldn't talk any sense into her.

Stuffed purple hippo in hand and a brown bag containing a tuna sandwich and a banana, Thrudi left the apartment.

Seconds later, there was a knock on the door.

It was Thrudi. "Can I take a root beer with me?"

The next morning, Mott was in the alley behind the apartment building with Fenris, trying to keep his snout away from a worm crawling along the pavement. Thrudi stood watch.

"Someone approaches," Thrudi said, wary.

A forest green SUV rolled up the alley and came to a stop. A sign on the door said, "Wolf Friends: Wolf Rescue & Rehabilitation."

Mott petted Fenris with last-minute desperation. His fur was so soft and clean under her fingers. His little tail wagged with energy and joy. His cute "mweeps" shattered her heart.

A woman with short silver hair and gold-wire glasses stepped out of the truck. Her eyes were kind, and she looked exactly like the kind of person who devoted their life to helping animals. Mott was disappointed. If the woman looked like a villain, Mott could have convinced herself that it was better to keep Fenris for his own good.

"I'm Bev. You must be Mott?" She addressed this to Thrudi, probably because Thrudi was standing and looking strong and powerful and in charge.

Mott raised her hand. "No, I'm Mott. That's Thrudi."

Bev stared at the sword handle poking from Thrudi's bag. "Is that sharp?"

"Very," Thrudi said.

"Cool. I have a nice collection. I'm into medieval stuff."

Now Thrudi stood there looking strong and powerful and confused.

"So that's the fluff, huh?" Bev gestured at Fenris, and her eyes got even a little kinder. "The shelter was right. He's definitely a wolf."

"Yes," Mott said. "That's why I can't keep him." Her voice shook a bit.

"You're doing a good thing, Mott. Thanks to you, he gets to run and hunt with his own kind, the way nature intended."

Mott knew this was true. She just wished it was easier to say goodbye.

"I must know more about this refuge of yours," Thrudi demanded. "Is it well hid? Does it rest between the branches of the world tree, inaccessible and guarded by terrible monsters that even the bravest god might dread?"

"It's in Idaho," Bev said. "Up in the mountains. We have a big spread."

"How far away is it?"

"Well, it took me a day and a night to drive here."

Thrudi was getting impatient. "But is Idaho in Midgard? Or Niflheim? Alfheim?"

"It's Idaho? The United States of America? About a thousand miles away, give or take." When Thrudi responded with only a frown, Bev shrugged her shoulders and started digging around in the back of her trunk.

"This Idaho place doesn't seem remote enough to hide a beast such as Fenris," Thrudi said to Mott. "But you and I will go with Bev and use Idaho as a starting point to find somewhere better concealed."

Ridiculous. First of all, why would Bev let them tag along? Also, Thrudi might be free to come and go between worlds, but Mott had a home and a mom and rules. Did they even have root beer in Idaho?

"Let's just get lil' fella into this—" Bev approached Fenris with a leash and collar in her hands.

"No, he hates leashes," Mott warned. "He'll run."

She was too late.

Fenris bolted as if he were strapped to a rocket engine. Before Mott could grab him, his fuzzy rear end was far down the alley and gaining distance, carried on stubby legs that shouldn't have been able to move so fast. Mott sprinted after him, and Thrudi took off after her.

"Fenris, stop!" Mott called when Fenris turned the corner at the end of the alley. "Stay! Heel! Bad wolf!"

Bev zoomed up in her truck a few seconds later. "Get in, girls! Quick!"

Thrudi and Mott piled into the front seat. Careful but

confident, Bev drove out of the alley and onto the street.

Mott caught a flash of tail rounding another corner. "There!"

"I see him," Bev said, pressing down the gas pedal. "Boy, he really doesn't like leashes, does he?"

"Who can blame him?" Thrudi said. "For on a lonely crag in turbulent seas, he was most cruelly bound by a ribbon as fine as silk but stronger than iron, forged by dwarven smiths from six impossible things, such as the bones of a mountain, and the breath of fish, and—"

"Thrudi." Mott elbowed her.

"Gleipnir," Thrudi finished stubbornly. "The ribbon's name was Gleipnir."

"There's the pup," Bev said with a triumphant grin, focused on the chase rather than what Thrudi was spouting. She turned another corner onto a road that dead-ended with a high concrete wall. Fenris stood, his neck craned to look up the wall.

"Let me get out," Mott said. "He trusts me."

Bev shook her head. "I want to get a little closer." She crept the truck forward, closing the distance to Fenrir.

Fenrir turned around to face the truck. His eyes were narrowed, his ears flattened, his teeth bared.

"Mott is right," said Thrudi. "Listen to her."

Bev didn't stop the truck, continuing to inch forward. "I just want to make sure he doesn't get past us."

Everything that happened next happened fast.

Fenris lowered himself into a crouch.

He launched into a run, charging the truck.

He opened his jaw, and that little mouth gaped impossibly wide, and Mott was again seized with the sensation of tumbling into a depthless gulf, falling into nothing.

She took a breath to clear her head, opened the door, shoved Thrudi out, and leaped after her.

A blast of wind whipped Mott's hair into her face, momentarily blocking her vision. The temperature dropped, sending a shivering ache into her bones. When she pushed her hair out of her face, the truck was gone.

Just . . . gone.

So was Bev.

And Fenris was a fuzzy puff, scampering away.

AFTER A FRUITLESS HALF-HOUR search on foot, Mott went home to fetch her bike. Thrudi sat on the handlebars while Mott pedaled and called out Fenris's name.

A row of parking meters down Culver Boulevard were snapped in half like pretzel sticks. Water geysered from a broken fire hydrant. And at the end of the block in front of a hair salon, a woman with wet hair and a plastic smock goggled at the stump of a palm tree.

"I wish to question that villager," Thrudi said, so Mott coasted to a stop. Reaching for her sword, Thrudi stomped toward the woman.

"Thrudi, no exposed swords," Mott called, following her. "It's unnecessary and dangerous and probably illegal."

"Next you'll tell me not to run with scissors."

"They have scissors in Asgard?"

"How else do you stab a dragon in the eye?" Thrudi stuffed her sword back in her bag. "Villager, tell us what has transpired here."

"It happened so fast," the woman blurted. "There was a whoosh and then . . ." She waved her arms around, gesturing at pretty much everything. "Maybe some kind of weird tornado or something."

Mott and Thrudi exchanged a knowing look.

Mott got back on her bike. "It seems like he's getting worse."

"He'll grow more destructive with every day, maybe every hour, just as the prophecy foretells."

"Or maybe he's just scared."

"Maybe both."

They resumed the search. There were more partially eaten trees, a parked car with a missing rear tire, a bus stop where Mott knew there ought to be a bench, but the trail of destruction ended after a few blocks.

"Do you think his stomach's full?" Mott asked.

Thrudi made a grim noise. "His ability to consume is limitless, and once you are pulled into his toothy maw, there is no escape. No object is too massive, too heavy, too strong to avoid falling inside him. He warps the very laws of nature. No human or god can resist the tide of his hunger."

"But he's cute," Mott felt the need to add in his defense.

"Oh, yes, he is adorable. And have you smelled him?"

"He smells great!"

"Like a mountain forest," Thrudi readily agreed.

Mott thought for a few seconds. "I have an idea how to find him. He can't just keep devouring parking meters and trees without people calling 911. I can check news and fire department reports on my phone."

She started searching. Right away, she found a bulletin. "The water tower at the movie studio just went missing," she told Thrudi. "The entire thing."

"I don't know what a movie studio is, but the way you use that device is marvelous. Is it magic? Are you a powerful sorcerer?"

Mott liked the idea of being a sorcerer. "Yes," she said. "Yes, I am. I am a very powerful sorcerer."

"Friend Mott, meeting you was good fortune."

Mott also liked how Thrudi had called her "friend." "Maybe . . . maybe we can hang out and do fun stuff if the world doesn't end?"

"I would like that," Thrudi said. "We could drink root beer. I could teach you sword combat, and you could teach me to use your magical device. Tell me, Mott, have you ever hunted wild boar?"

"I'm not sure I'd enjoy that? Have you ever ridden a roller coaster? It's a cart that goes around curves really fast and sometimes upside down and makes you scream.

"That sounds frightening," Thrudi said.

"I know! That's why it's fun."

"I see. Much like getting gored by a boar tusk."

Yes, it would be fun being Thrudi's friend, Mott decided. They had a lot they could teach each other.

When they reached the movie studio, Thrudi regarded the tall, windowless buildings stretching down the block. "This is quite a fortress. How many warriors lie within?"

"It's not a fortress. They film movies and TV shows in there."

"What are those?"

"You know, stories acted out for entertainment? What's entertainment like where you're from?"

"Usually it's just one person reciting a tale of heroism. But sometimes there's a human sacrifice. Those are popular."

"There's no way my mom would let me watch a human sacrifice."

"She sounds very strict."

"I guess?"

"Can you use your device to fly us over the wall as birds? Or perhaps allow us to pass through it as though it were but insubstantial mist?"

"It's really mostly just for looking stuff up. If this was a fortress, how would you get in?"

"I'd lead an overwhelming force of berserkers and slaughter anyone who stood in my way."

"Thrudi, I'm serious, you cannot go around slaughtering people in my world. It's considered wrong. You have to promise me. Zero slaughtering."

Thrudi's shoulders slumped. "Anyway, we lack an army of berserkers."

"We won't need them. I just came up with a plan."

Down the block, a line of cars waited to enter the lot. One of them was a pickup truck with an open bed.

Mott leaned her bike against the wall.

She loved her bike, one of the most precious things she'd brought with her from Pennsylvania. Two years ago, her dad had promised to send her a bike for her birthday, and he'd actually kept that promise, only the bike that got delivered was for a little kid. It even had training wheels. It was like her dad didn't know her at all. But Mott's mom had made that bike go away, and one day Mott came home from school to find a new red bike in the kitchen. It wasn't the most expensive bike, but it was hers. Mott knew it wasn't magic that had made it appear, but her mom working overtime to make enough money to buy it.

"I guess I'll have to leave it here," she said. "It'll probably get stolen."

"The bonds of kinship among people break. It is foretold in the prophecy."

Mott opened her notebook to the Ragnarok page and drew a question mark next to "The bonds of kinship break." Could a stolen bike be part of the end of the world? If you couldn't leave your bike without someone stealing it, maybe it meant the world hadn't been right for a long time.

The pickup truck crept down the line of traffic, and it was a simple job to sneak up behind it, step on the rear bumper, and fall into the back. Mott pulled a paint-spattered tarp over them, and they lay quiet as the truck pulled up to the guard gate.

If Mott could have forgotten about Fenris being in trouble, and forgotten about the end of the world, this might have been fun. She'd never been on an adventure before.

The truck pulled forward past the gate. It continued at a slow pace, and Mott and Thrudi hopped out.

Golf carts puttered between old-timey office buildings and along clean grass-belted sidewalks with light posts that looked like gas lamps. Tourists followed a guide like a flock of ducklings as she pointed out buildings that had appeared in TV shows and movies. People went in and out of the buildings, most of them regular-looking office workers but a few in costumes: a cowboy, a woman in an astronaut space suit, a couple of clowns.

"Oh, look at that guy in the black armor," Mott said. "He must be on a sci-fi show."

"His armor looks thin and crackable," Thrudi judged.

"Okay, how about her?" A woman in a beautiful ball gown and sneakers rushed by them.

"That is a lovely dress. Although not suited to weather or combat."

"What about that guy?" Mott pointed to a man across a lawn. His costume was impressive, rusty chain mail splattered in very convincing dried blood. One arm was concealed under a cape of white fur, while his exposed arm rippled with muscle. And in a fist the size of a pumpkin, he gripped an ax big enough to fell a large tree with one blow.

He scanned the crowd, looking for . . . something.

Mott found she couldn't keep her eyes on him for long without getting a bit of the Grand Canyon feeling.

"That's Tew," Thrudi rasped, her eyes wide, her flesh paper white. "A god of war."

Slowly, like a rotating planet, he began turning his head in their direction.

Thrudi reached for her sword.

"Prop girl," a man in a golf cart shouted. "Why aren't you on set? Didn't you hear about the water tower thing? We had to move the production to Soundstage Two. We're about to shoot the final battle, and we need every sword!"

"Uh . . . ?" Thrudi said.

"We're late, let's go." Mott shoved Thrudi into the back seat of the cart and piled in after her.

The cart lurched down the road.

Tew, the war god, wasn't following. He was still back behind them, searching.

It was a short drive to a windowless concrete box of a building with a plaque over the door reading "Soundstage 2." And next to the door, on the asphalt ground, sat a fuzzy white wolf pup.

Fenris was licking the building's outer wall.

He was tasting it.

Mott leaped from the cart before it even came to a full stop. "Fenris, don't you dare!"

Fenris turned with a startled mweep. Seeing Mott, he ran to her with his tail a wagging blur.

"You are naughty," Mott scolded, scooping him up. "Did you eat those parking meters? And a tree? And a water tower?"

Fenris whined and tried to hide his face in Mott's armpit.

"Mott." Thrudi pointed down the road with her sword. "Tew is coming. We must either confront him or conceal ourselves."

"I'm the animal wrangler," Mott explained to the production assistant. "This dog is in the movie, and I am wrangling him."

"Fine, whatever," the assistant said. "Let's go."

The building was a single vast room, like a barn or an

airplane hangar, with lights suspended from catwalks overhead. Technicians rushed around, moving more lights and huge cameras on wheels and microphones hanging from poles.

Mott took it all in, spellbound. She could only imagine the epic root beer reviews she could film with all this equipment and crew.

Someone with a megaphone was trying to organize a horde of barbarians in front of a bright green wall. The barbarians carried axes and spears and swords and wore spiky armor and horned helmets.

Thrudi laughed. "Those helmets are ridiculous."

"They're costume helmets," Mott said. "All those guys are actors. The weapons aren't real."

"Ah, so they are making a story."

"That's right."

"What's the story about?"

"It's about *me*!" boomed a voice. "*Star Hammer: The Motion Picture*, starring *me* as Star Hammer!" A tall grinning man strode across the soundstage, casually tossing and catching a massive hammer. He was dressed similarly to the other barbarians, with shiny blond hair cascading over his gleaming chrome shoulder plates.

Mott's heart pounded with excitement. "That's . . . that's Chris Hevans!"

Thrudi tightened her grip on her sword. "Is he dangerous? Should I slay him?"

"No, he's a movie star! My mom loves him! I wonder if I can get an autograph—"

"Puppy!" Chris Hevans's bright blue eyes went wide. He rushed up to Fenris. "Oh, gosh, what a cute little thing. Is he real? Or is he a puppet? Can I hold him?"

Fenris drooled a little.

"I don't think that would be a good idea," Mott said.

Chris Hevans's face fell. "Doesn't he like people?"

"He likes people," said Thrudi. "He likes everything. Trees, vehicles, minions of Tew—"

"Chris," the man with the megaphone called, "we're ready for you."

"That's *me*," he explained to Mott and Thrudi unnecessarily. "Chris Hevans, starring as Star Hammer, in *Star Hammer: The Motion Picture*!" He flexed his arms, threw his head back in a hearty laugh, and strode over to the green wall.

Mott scritched Fenris's head. "Good boy for not eating an A-list movie star."

Fenris sighed.

The man with the megaphone—the director, Mott assumed—was calling out instructions. "Okay, everyone, here's how this is going to go. Chris, you stand there . . . no, a little right, good, good, brilliant. Barbarians, on 'Action!' you're going to charge Chris. Then Chris is going to bring his hammer down. That's the cue for the pyrotechnics."

A woman in a baseball hat with "BOOM" printed on it raised her hand. She stood at a table before a black box with a bunch of complicated-looking controls and one big red switch.

"There'll be flame and smoke and sparks," the director continued. "The barbarians fall back, and then Chris—"

"Then Chris Hevans strikes his mighty pose!" said Chris Hevans, striking a mighty pose.

"Right," the director went on. "Chris strikes the pose, and we cut. Everyone got it? Okay, quiet on set! Aaaaand . . . action!"

The barbarians roared and brandished their fake weapons and began their charge.

"Why do you still have the sword?" It was the production assistant, whispering angrily at Thrudi. "Why is the sword not on set?"

"It's for the next scene," Mott said.

"And you!" the production assistant whispered, a little louder, a little angrier. "Why aren't *you* on set?"

He wasn't talking to Mott.

She felt something. A presence. A cold sensation in her bones. A heavy sadness. A roar in her ears like people crying out in pain. She knew Tew was behind her even before she saw him.

"He's in the next scene, too," she said weakly.

Thrudi raised her blade, a grim, tight-lipped smile on her brave face. A strand of sweat traced a line down her neck.

"You had no hope of eluding me," Tew said in a voice like cannon fire. "I am war itself, bringer of strife and glory." He gestured at Fenris with his bloodstained ax. "And that beast is my weapon."

"He's just rehearsing," Mott told the production assistant.

The production assistant shook his head and walked away, muttering, "I can't believe they pay people to write this stuff."

Tew lifted his ax. It shouldn't have cast a shadow as big as it did. The light wasn't right, and it wasn't large enough, but it was as if the moon had eclipsed the sun.

Thrudi readied herself.

"Fenris, run!" Mott said.

Fenris took off like a shot. And even though Mott had no weapon, she moved between Tew and the pup. She didn't do so without thinking. This was not instinct. It was a deliberate decision, and she was so terrified she thought she might barf up her own heart. But she'd promised to protect Fenris.

Tew didn't even notice. He sidestepped her, ducked under Thrudi's swinging sword, and gave pursuit.

Fenris aimed for the set where the barbarians were running toward Chris Hevans, who was still posing. It took Tew only two strides to cover the distance. He lifted his ax high above his head at the exact same time that Chris Hevans raised his hammer.

Fenris ran between the legs of the barbarians, tripping some, who fell into others, and soon there was a messy tangle of stumbling actors.

"Hey, what . . . ?" screamed the director. Confused camera operators and lighting and sound technicians and pretty much everyone on set looked like they had no idea what was going on and what they were supposed to do.

Fenris leaped into the air.

"Nooooo," Mott screamed as the wolf stretched his jaws and fell upon Chris Hevans.

It was like a magic trick. Like a snake rapidly swallowing something bigger than itself. Chris Hevans's head went in Fenris's mouth. Then his broad shoulders. His massive chest. His entire torso, his waist, hips, legs, boots. By the time Fenris landed on his paws, Chris Hevans was gone.

But Tew was not.

His blade reflected the studio lights in a brilliant, bloody glare. The same glare shone in his eyes. He was going to get Fenris. He was going to use Fenris as a weapon to bring about chaos and destruction. And Mott had no doubt he would hurt Fenris in the process.

Thrudi surged to block Tew from getting to Fenris, but she wasn't fast enough.

Mott would have to be faster.

She leaped to the table where the pyrotechnician in the "BOOM" hat was stationed. Mott reached across her and flipped the big red switch. A blast went off, right beneath Tew's feet. He flew back in a ball of flame and smoke and sparks and crashed hard onto the studio floor.

Mott sprinted for Fenris, who, despite some smoke stains on his fur, was contentedly licking his chops.

Scooping him up, she leaped over Tew's stunned and groaning form and raced out the soundstage door.

"Mweep?" Fenris said. He blinked with innocence.

8

"SOMEONE STOLE MY BIKE."

Mott stared at the now empty space. Blinking away tears, she drew a big ugly checkmark next to "Men forget the bonds of kinship" on her Ragnarok list.

"I am sorry, Mott," Thrudi said.

"It's my fault. I should have found something to chain it to."

"We shouldn't need chains to make people behave."

Fenris mweeped in agreement.

Mott's phone played a few notes of the Urpshchmidt root beer jingle, signaling a text from her mom. It was their noontime check-in. Mott sniffed. "My mom's asking me how I am. And where I am. And what I'm doing."

"Are you going to tell her?"

"That I got chased by a war god with an ax in a movie studio?"

"Whenever I didn't want my parents to know my whereabouts I'd tell them I almost drowned in the creek. Then I'd throw myself in the creek to make it convincing. This one time I got washed so far downstream I ended up in the land of frost giants. That part was hard to explain."

"Doing okay," Mott typed. "I'm outside. Thinking about Chris Hevans movies. Love you."

All of which was nearly true.

Her mom texted back some hearts.

Thrudi glanced around, uneasy. "We should try to get some distance from Tew."

"But he got blown up. Isn't that going to at least slow him down?"

"One time I saw an entire ox fall on him and he paused only long enough to comb his hair."

"I have questions."

"The important question is how are we going to travel at speed without your bike. Perhaps we can find a steed. At home I have a horse named Slashhoof. That's because she uses her hooves to slash. Why, this one time I was fighting a troll, and Slashhoof kicked him in the neck and his head came clean off." She chuckled fondly at the memory.

"I don't think there're any horse stables around here," Mott said with secret relief.

"It doesn't have to be a horse. A large stag would do. Perhaps a sturdy goat."

Mott checked her phone. "Sorry, no farms in this neighborhood either."

Thrudi gestured at the passing cars. "What about one of those smoke-breathing four-wheeled chariots, then?"

"I don't have a driver's license," said Mott. "Also, I don't know how to drive. Also, and this is important, grand theft auto is against the law."

Thrudi's face brightened. "Oh, but what about *that*?"

That turned out to be a red motor scooter puttering down the street.

"We'd still need a permit to ride it and . . ."

Thrudi wasn't listening. She charged into the road, right in the scooter's path.

Eep eep, went the scooter's little horn. The rider, a small-ish, old-ish man, braked to a halt. Cars honked and swerved around.

"What's wrong with you?" the old-ish man shouted. "Get out of the road."

"I offer you my greetings," Thrudi said with fanfare. "I am Thrudi, Valkyrie of Asgard. My companion and I wish to purchase your steed."

"My . . . ? I don't have a steed."

"I apologize for miscommunicating. I refer to your magical device. The one you're straddling."

"Is this slang? Are you . . . are you a Zoomer?"

"I don't think so," Thrudi said. "Mott, am I Zoomer?"

Mott stepped into the road. "What she means is, we would like to buy your scooter."

"It's not for sale," he said. "I need it to transport my cabbages." The basket behind the scooter's saddle was full of grocery bags, which were, indeed, full of cabbages.

Thrudi began rummaging in her duffel bag.

"No swords!" Mott shouted.

Both Thrudi and the old man looked at her as if she'd lost her mind.

Thrudi continued reaching into her bag until she pulled out a little leather pouch. From the pouch, she produced seven thick gold coins.

The old man's eyes popped.

Thrudi dropped them in the man's palms. He held them up to the sun. He scratched them with a fingernail. He bit them.

Saying nothing, he lowered the kickstand, gathered his cabbages, and skipped down the sidewalk, a blissful smile on his face.

Thrudi watched him go. "I paid too much, didn't I?"

Mott tried to guess how much root beer Thrudi's gold might have bought. "At least now we have a steed. It needs a name."

"Oh! Slashhoof Two!"

"Maybe just Scooty?"

"Very well. Scooty. And now we should go before Tew recovers."

Mott put Fenris in the basket and climbed on. "Where to?"

Thrudi got on behind her. "Friend Mott, how would you feel about meeting another god?"

"Not too great, to be honest." But she keyed the engine on.

Thrudi knocked on the chipped-paint door of a yellow house on a quiet block in Venice. The door opened, revealing a tall, lean man with chapped lips and eyes the color of granite. His flesh was ice with a bloom of color in his cheeks that looked like lava, and Mott was gripped by a little of that spiraling Grand Canyon sensation.

"Scouts," he said. "Fantastic. Do you have cookies? I'll take twelve boxes of Thin Mints, please." His voice was rough, as if he had sand in his throat.

Thrudi bowed. "Great Hermod, messenger of the Aesir, I am the shield-maiden Thrudi. My companion is Mott, a cunning sorceress of this world. We come to you for counsel in a time of strife."

Hermod's face fell. "So, no cookies then?"

"Sorry," Mott said.

Fenris sat obediently at Mott's feet. Hermod cocked his head at him. Fenris cocked his head in return. A look of recognition dawned on Hermod's face.

"Is that . . . ?"

"He is," confirmed Thrudi.

"Get in before someone sees." Hermod stepped back to let Mott and Thrudi inside, scanning the street before shutting the door.

Mott had never given much thought to what a god's living room might look like, but this wasn't it. He had a wall completely covered with newspaper and magazine clippings. The headlines were all about climate and weather and natural disasters: ice storms and droughts and heat waves and typhoons and blizzards and hurricanes, photos of people standing on the roofs of drowned neighborhoods, flattened downtowns, dry and barren wastelands, pine trees going up in flames like birthday candles. Red strands of yarn held in place by pins drew connections between the clippings.

In movies, people who had walls like this were always paranoid conspiracy nuts. They believed the government knew about UFOs and that Bigfoot was a space alien superspy.

Mott thought about the journal in her pocket, with her list of stuff like tidal waves and weird chickens.

"How did you find me?" Hermod asked Thrudi.

"I had heard you forsook Asgard for this world long ago. But I'm not the one who found you. The sorceress did."

Mott showed him her phone screen. "Your address is listed. See? Hermod, 501 South Venice Avenue."

Hermod scratched the stubble on his chin. "I don't remember listing myself. I bet Loki did that. I can't stand tricksters. They're lying shape-changers, and they think they're so funny." He regarded Fenris, who was gazing around, looking for something to eat. "What do you want from me?"

"We have pledged to protect Fenris, and we were

hoping you might advise us."

"My advice is never pledge to protect Fenris."

"You are the farthest-traveled of the gods," Thrudi pressed on. "Surely you must know of a refuge, a hideaway, somewhere to keep Fenris safe from Tew. Perhaps Helheim?"

Hermod plopped down on the couch. "You want wise counsel, and you didn't even bring me cookies. Look, say you got him to the underworld, what difference would it make? The moon also exists in Helheim. He'll still eat it. He'll still eat Odin. Vidar will still kill the wolf. And everything will come crashing down, the end. Nothing you can do about it. The wolf is as doomed as the rest of us."

Mott bristled. "I'm going to keep my promise."

Hermod smiled sadly. "You may believe that, sorceress, but you're young, and there are other promises hanging over your head older than you can imagine." He turned to Thrudi. "Have you told her of Ragnarok?"

"She mostly learned about it on her own."

Hermod stretched his long legs out on the coffee table. The soles of his dusty boots were worn thin, as if he'd walked a million miles in them. "It might be interesting, seeing Fenris eat the moon. Will it just disappear—there one moment, and in the next, an empty space in the sky? Will the earth's rotation change? Will mountains shift like pies sliding down a tilted table? Will the ocean spill like water out of a tub and wash this whole mess away? Or will lunar crumbs fall to Earth, hammers from the sky, triggering continent-shattering tremors, igniting volcanoes and sending flames and life-choking smoke into the air? What will it look like when the gods and the monsters fight against such a background, their battle laying waste to anything left alive? Yes, it should be interesting. Not so much when he eats the sun. That's just showing off."

"Please," Mott said. "There must be something we can do."

"Maybe there was, long ago, before Tew fed him the Annihilation Rune."

"Fed him the what?" Thrudi said.

Hermod raised an eyebrow. "They didn't teach you that in Valkyrie school? Here, I'll show you. Got anything to write with?"

Mott passed him her root beer journal and pen. He flipped to a blank page and drew some symbols. The lines on the page faded, and in their place was the image of an island. Not a drawing, but real, as if the journal had become a window. The island was not much more than a sharp slab of rock piercing a raging black sea. Through the ocean spray, Mott could make out the figure of Tew, looming over a much smaller creature: Fenris.

Shivering, the image of Fenris hunched miserably, his fur sticky with salt water, his legs bound with a shimmering ribbon that hurt Mott's eyes to look at.

Tew loomed over the pup, red light spilling between the fingers of his closed fist. "Do you know what this is, wolf?" His voice was like the deep cracking of a great tree right before it falls. He opened his hand and lying flat on his palm was a rectangular object the size of a domino, glowing like an ember. Etched on its face was a black double-loop—the infinity symbol—with a deep mark slashed diagonally across it. "This took the best smiths in Svartalfheim centuries to craft. It is the Annihilation Rune, and hammered into its fabric is the embodiment of wreckage, of death, of pain."

He placed it on the ground before Fenris.

"Eat it," Tew commanded.

"Mweep," Fenris whimpered.

"Eat it," Tew said again, more forcefully.

Fenris's eyes narrowed. "Mweep," he said, with a clear edge of defiance.

Tew grunted, his eyes locked on Fenris's. He sighed. "The rune is ammunition, and you will be my weapon. Together, we will end worlds."

Fenris pulled his lips back in a snarl. His teeth flashed like lightning, and his growl seemed to come from deep within the earth. The island shuddered; the waves churned.

Tew closed his eyes. "Very well," he said.

With quick, violent movements, he gripped Fenris's jaws in his hands and forced them open. Fenris struggled to resist, but Tew clutched the rune in one hand and forced it down Fenris's throat.

Fenris convulsed and coughed and bit down. Tew shrieked. He tried to withdraw his hand from Fenris's mouth, but his wrist ended in bone and blood and chewed meat.

Tew's face twisted in what was either a grimace of pain or a triumphant smile. "Do you feel it yet?" he croaked. "The inferno raging inside? An insatiable appetite for devastation? Or are you too simple a creature to understand what you are now becoming? Before, you were a pathetic creature with nothing more than the prophecy's promise that you would grow strong. But now, thanks to me, you will become unstoppable. You will become horrible. You will become great. Perhaps you will thank me."

Fenris's stomach rumbled. The ground shuddered.

"When there have been three winters in Asgard with no summer between, I will come back for you." Tew wrapped the stump of his wrist in his fur cloak. "And then, little wolf, then will come the age of wolves, until the world goes down."

Fenris mweeped.

The images faded, and the lines on the blank page returned. Hermod gave Mott her journal back.

She was out of breath. "Tew did this to Fenris? He made him this way?"

"Just as I showed you."

"But . . . why?"

"Something as big as the end of the worlds doesn't just happen. Ragnarok may be inevitable, but it's inevitable because of the things people did. The choices they made. Tew put the rune inside Fenris to make sure Ragnarok would happen."

Mott saw an opportunity. "What if we got the rune out of Fenris? Then Ragnarok wouldn't happen, right? We could save the worlds?"

"Turn back a disaster that's been brewing for thousands of years? You? A little girl from Midgard and a wayward

Valkyrie? It doesn't sound very likely."

"But is it *possible*?"

Hermod did something with his eyebrows that suggested a shrug. "Who can say? Maybe you can rid Fenris of the rune, but that would mean slicing him open. That generally kills creatures. You'd be breaking your promise to take care of him."

Thrudi frowned as though she were concentrating on a math problem. "Fenris's life, or the universe . . ."

"Thrudi!" Mott said, shocked. "Don't even say it."

"She's just speaking the truth," Hermod said, tired. "You made a promise without knowing what you were promising. How determined are you to keep your oath?"

"Very."

"Anyway, no matter what you choose, failure is certain. Because the universe keeps its promises."

Mott started for the door. "We'll see about that."

9

FENRIS GROWLED ON MOTT'S LAP while Thrudi flipped through an issue of *Fancy Poodle* magazine. It was a busy day at the veterinarian's office, and the waiting room was packed. A worried-looking man cradled a fishbowl containing a ceramic castle and a very orange goldfish. Something in a cat carrier hissed at Fenris. And a figure draped in hand-knitted shawls balanced a big wire cage on her lap. Inside the cage was a big, beautiful rooster with shining feathers of gold.

A TV blared news of doom all over the world.

Brush fires raged in Australia.

A devastating tsunami pummeled Sumatra.

Warming water temperatures were killing coral reefs

in the Indian ocean, turning them as white and lifeless as corpses.

"Aren't you going to check any of these off in your book?" asked Thrudi. "Surtur, flame-wielding, sets the land on fire?"

With a sigh, Mott got out her notebook. She missed the days when she used it for root beer reviews. She checked off another bullet point.

"What about the coral reefs?" Thrudi said.

"What about them? That's not part of Ragnarok."

"The world-spanning serpent, venom-spitting?"

"I already checked him off for the rising waters."

"Good. And what about him?" Thrudi gestured at the rooster.

"He's just a chicken, Thrudi. Not everything is about—"

Just then, the rooster cock-a-doodled his head off.

The cats yowled, and the goldfish hid in its castle.

"Okay, okay," Mott relented, checking off "The golden rooster crows to summon the gods."

The next story on the news was about massive hail-storms in Germany. Mott hoped Amanda was okay.

A woman in a ponytail and a white doctor's coat came into the waiting room. "I understand you have some kind of emergency with this cute guy?"

Mott stood. "My dog ate something he shouldn't have."

"Oh, no. What was it?"

"The Rune of Annihilation," Thrudi supplied. "It is an object of tremendous power, and it drives Fenris to destroy all you know and love."

"The Rune of . . . is this some kind of Dungeons and Dragons thing? Like a figurine?"

"Something like that," Mott said.

"How long ago?"

"Thousands of years by your reckoning," said Thrudi.

"Wow, you kids have imagination. Come with me."

In the back room, Mott's eyes went to the vet's collection of surgical scalpels and long-bladed scissors and sharp picks.

"Can you make him throw up the rune, or do you have to do surgery?" Mott asked. She hoped Fenris wouldn't need surgery, but if that's what it took to get the Annihilation Rune out of him, she'd make sure it got done by a professional. "We have money, so we can pay you."

Thrudi reached into her bag for her pouch of gold coins, but the vet waved her off.

"Let's see what we're dealing with first." She got out an electric razor. "I'm going to shave his belly to get an ultrasound image and see what's inside him."

"He won't like that," Mott warned. But she was wrong. Fenris happily lay on his back and wiggled his little paws while the vet ran the razor over his belly.

"Back home they shave with axes," Thrudi exclaimed, amazed. "One time Egil the Fearless was getting his beard trimmed and the barber sneezed, and after that he was Egil the Faceless."

The vet shook her head and laughed. "I love how much thought you put into your games." After smearing some gel on Fenris's pink, naked tummy, she wheeled over a cart with a laptop kind of thing connected by a cable to a hand-held gadget. She passed the gadget over Fenris's abdomen.

"Do you see the rune?" Mott asked.

"Also, please look for a dead man's hand," added Thrudi.

The vet grunted. She pressed a few keys on the laptop thing and ran the scanner over Fenris's belly again. "I'm not seeing *anything*," she said slowly. "No esophagus, no intestines, no stomach."

Mott peered at the screen. It displayed a black field, blacker than if the machine was turned off, blacker than the darkest night sky Mott had ever seen, like the bottom of an impossibly deep well.

Staring at it, Mott got that sideways Grand Canyon

sensation again. She wasn't the only one. Thrudi swayed on her feet and gripped Mott's shoulder to keep herself steady. The vet let out a long-held breath, as if she'd forgotten how to breathe.

"The machine must be broken," she said shakily. She checked all the cable connections and slapped the scanner against her palm before trying again.

If anything, the image was even darker now. It showed a profound nothingness that Mott knew in her gut she was not supposed to be seeing.

This is what Fenris contained. He was no puppy. He was no wolf. He was a force of nature, a black hole, a universe with nothing in it, and he wanted to turn everything in existence into the same nothingness.

Mott was close to begging the vet to stop scanning him when she finally pulled the scanner away.

The vet swallowed. "Broken," she rasped.

"Can you help him?" Mott asked.

"Broken," the vet said again, this time barely audible.

Fenris blepped his tongue. "Mweep."

Mott put Fenris in Scooty's basket and sat on the cold, drizzle-dampened saddle, her hand on the ignition but not turning it. "Now what?" she said, forlorn.

Thrudi looked just as dismal as Mott felt. "We need to know where Tew is. He's surely recovered from the explosion by now. He'll be searching for us."

Mott got out her phone. "Well, if a god of war is stomping around LA, someone's going to notice."

Thrudi's eyes were full of wonder as she watched Mott thumb buttons on her phone screen. "The ability to track a god is truly mighty."

"You know, it's not really magic. It's just a phone. Lots of people have them. I'm not a sorcerer."

"Just because magic is plentiful in your realm doesn't mean it's not magic."

"Oh, here, a post on NeighborSnoop: 'Has anyone else seen a strange man dressed in rusty chain mail turning over full-sized garbage dumpsters? This just happened in the alley behind my house. Last saw him heading north up Abbot-Kinney Avenue. Seemed very angry. He makes me nervous because he has a gigantic, bloodstained ax.'"

"That is definitely Tew," Thrudi said.

"Abbot-Kinney's not far from here, so let's go in the opposite direction."

She started the motor, and suddenly her bones ached

with cold. A man approached, his eyes the color of fresh snow, lashes dusted with frost. He was dressed like Tew, furs and leathers, with a huge sword hanging from a broad belt. His right boot was just a boot, but his left boot was a bulky mass of mismatched leather patches, black and brown and some the color of scabs.

Fenris buried his face in his basket.

"Vidar," breathed Thrudi.

"Valkyrie," he whispered, fog curling from the corner of his mouth. "I hear you had a skirmish with Tew and survived. That's a job well done. You should be proud of yourself."

"Thank you."

Since they were being polite to each other, Mott figured she'd better behave the same way. "Your shoe is cool," she squeaked.

Vidar smiled thinly, an expression that somehow made his face colder. "It took a long time to craft. It's made from the scraps of a thousand generations of shoemakers. It has to be tough, you see, because I'll be planting my foot on Fenris's lower jaw, and then stretching his mouth open and driving my sword down his throat."

There was no anger in his voice. No emotion at all. He

was just reciting some facts.

Thrudi went for her sword.

"Please don't," Vidar warned. "I dislike hurting children."

"Then why not choose to help us?" Thrudi said, desperation in her voice. "Tew wants to use Fenris as a weapon. People are going to get hurt. You could—"

Vidar shook his head. "There's nothing you or I can do to prevent it. We all have a part to play in the prophecy. There must be war. There must be strife. Fenris must eat the sun and moon. And I must play my part as well, for I am Vidar, son of Odin, and the prophecy says Fenris dies at my hands. It's really not that complicated. Everyone has a job to do. Will you give me the monster?"

"No," Mott said. Her voice shook with nerves. "If we all have a role, then protecting Fenris is mine." She pulled back on the accelerator, and with a squeal of tires, the scooter jolted into motion.

She zigzagged around garbage cans, down an alley, and made a sharp turn onto a side street she didn't even know the name of. Did the prophecy mention anything about her crashing into a parked car, or a guy crossing the street and not looking for traffic because he was on his phone? All of which nearly happened.

"How fast can gods run?" Mott asked, checking her little round side mirror.

"As fast they need to," said Thrudi.

Vidar's mismatched boots made his stride a little awkward, but it didn't seem to slow him down. He was right behind them.

Mott made a hard left and accelerated when they reached Abbot-Kinney. The scooter's motor whined as the speedometer meter climbed past thirty miles per hour. Abbot-Kinney was a busy street lined with boutiques and galleries and cafés. Cars slowed down to find parking spaces, buses blocked traffic, and jaywalkers darted into the road. Making things worse, the drizzle had ramped up to a full downpour, and the street was starting to flood, water rising up the curbs. Mott's toes felt like ice. Water streamed from her hair into her eyes.

Fenris mweeped in the basket, high and sharp.

"Is he okay?" Mott asked.

"Indeed, I believe he is enjoying this. By the way, Vidar is gaining and he has drawn his sword."

In the mirror, Vidar was close enough that she could see his facial expression. He didn't look angry. He just looked determined, as if he knew it was only a matter of time before he caught them.

Mott coaxed more speed out of Scooty. With cars clogging traffic and entire lakes of rain-filled potholes, she was shocked she hadn't crashed yet.

"Thrudi, can you read English?" Mott asked, weaving around cars.

"Yes, we Valkyries are schooled in all the languages of the nine realms."

"Good. Can you get my phone out of my right pocket?"

"Your magic device? Yes, I think . . . got it."

"Okay, I need to keep my hands on the handlebars and my eyes on the road, so you're going to have to do some magic."

"But I'm not a wizard."

"It's okay; I'm going to walk you through this spell." Mott told Thrudi which buttons and icons to press to bring up NeighborSnoop.

"I'm doing it!" Thrudi said. "I'm doing magic! I'm a wizard, Mott!"

"Is there anything else about Tew? Or anyone with an ax tossing trash dumpsters?"

"I see a dancing cat. It's talented."

"What?"

"Oh," said Thrudi. "I think I pressed the wrong thing. Tell me again how to cast the spell?"

Mott repeated the instructions.

"Let's see . . . something about a missing turtle. Something about a stolen package. Something about a suspicious brown-skinned person . . ."

Mott rolled her eyes. "Sounds racist. Anything else?"

"Oh, here . . . A man in armor and furs picking up a parked car and tossing it into the road on Oh-lime-pick Boulevard."

"Olympic? We can be there in a minute."

"If Tew's there, then why are we . . . ?"

There was no time to explain. In the mirror, Vidar was closing the distance.

Mott squeezed a little more speed from the scooter.

Up ahead in the intersection, flinging aside a manhole cover and peering down the hole, was Tew. His cheeks were blackened from the pyrotechnic blast at the studio, and his eyes red-rimmed. The effects of the blast only made him look fiercer. He rose to his full height when he saw the scooter bearing down on him and hefted his ax.

Mott twisted Scooty's right handlebar grip all the way back. The engine whined, and Scooty bravely reached maximum speed.

Tew grinned.

Mott aimed for him.

"Aha! I get it!" Thrudi clapped Mott on the back with excitement. "Tew wants to abduct Fenris to use as a weapon, while Vidar pursues us because he wants to kill Fenris, because he's so unimaginative he believes the only thing he can do is play his part in the prophecy. So you're going to weaponize their opposite goals and make them face each other. Brilliant!"

"Aw, thanks!" Mott said, glowing. "And you're good at explaining things!"

"I appreciate it."

"We're probably going to die."

"Oh, definitely," Thrudi agreed.

"Hold on!" Mere feet from the reach of Tew's swinging ax, Mott slammed the brakes and steered right. The tires slid, and Mott had to put her foot to the pavement to keep Scooty upright. Vidar stumbled to avoid running full-tilt into the back of the scooter and ran into Tew.

With the scooter wobbling, Mott turned the throttle all the way and kept going.

The clang of Vidar's sword against Tew's ax sent spikes of pain into Mott's molars.

The road surface shuddered and cracked. Brakes squealed

as cars swerved to avoid the battling gods. One car jumped the curb and collided into a fire hydrant, sending up a pillar of water. People on the sidewalk scrambled for their lives.

The gods did battle, and Mott focused on the road ahead, leaving destruction behind. She shivered as the scooter fled through the rain, aimed for the questionable safety of home.

10

HEAVY CLOUDS BOMBED THE EARTH with rain. Mott didn't know if the booms rocking the sky were thunder or the din of Tew and Vidar fighting. Fenris tried to bite raindrops as if they were bees. Drenched and miserable, Mott steered Scooty home. By the time she and Thrudi arrived, their shoes squelched like sponges, but at least, according to NeighborSnoop, they were miles away from battling gods.

Thrudi hesitated when Mott went through the apartment complex's front gate. "I will remain outside and stand guard."

"Don't be weird. It's a firehose out here. Come inside with me."

"You must remember, Mott, I am accustomed to harsh environs. I should tell you about the time I fell down a well full of snakes."

"There's water in my pants, Thrudi! Come inside!"

Thrudi considered. "Very well, I suppose I can be on guard for angry gods indoors. But I will remain hidden from your mother, as must Fenris. Perhaps you can roll us up in a rug?"

Mott grabbed Thrudi's wrist and pulled her through the gate. "We'll have to hide Fenris in my room, but I'll tell my mom you're a friend who needs a place to stay the night. She'll have a few questions, and she might ask to talk to your parents. But she'll let you stay. Okay?"

Thrudi didn't answer, and Mott got the feeling she'd brought up a sensitive topic.

Soon, they were in dry T-shirts and sweatpants, and Thrudi's furs and leathers were clanking around downstairs in the building's laundry room.

"I hope your stuff doesn't get ruined in the dryer," Mott said, heating up two mugs of cocoa in the microwave.

"I don't mind wearing your clothes. They allow great freedom of movement." Thrudi practiced sword lunges until Mott handed her a mug.

"This is amazing!" Thrudi said after a sip. "So warm! And rich! Mott, my sorcerous friend, this beverage is magical!"

"Oh, that's right, you've never had chocolate before."

"Where I come from the most hallowed warriors drink mead straight from the udder of the goat Heidrún. It's not as good as your chocolate drink. This is almost as good as root beer."

Mott smiled, pleased. Thrudi liked Mott's clothes. She liked hot chocolate. And she really liked root beer. She liked the things Mott liked, and it made Mott feel as though Thrudi might like her, too.

"I wish we could just hang out and do stuff," said Mott.

"What kind of stuff?"

"I don't know. Watch Chris Hevans movies. Or you could review root beer with me on my root beer channel. Or you could teach me how to use a sword."

Thrudi wiped a hot chocolate mustache off her lips. "That sounds like good stuff. Yes, Mott, perhaps one day."

A happy Fenris thumped his tail on the kitchen floor.

After such a harrowing two days, it was nice to be with a friend and a cute pup and pretend everything was normal and safe, even if just for a few minutes.

The rasp of a key sliding into the front doorknob ruined the illusion.

"Oh! We have to hide Fenris. And come up with a reason why you have a sharp, bladed weapon."

"Just hide us both," Thrudi said. "I'll be fine. Why, this one time I remained concealed in a hollow tree for four days. Which would have been fine had it not been for the bees—"

"Quick, this way." Mott managed to usher Thrudi and Fenris into her bedroom and shut the door behind them just as her mom's voice sounded from the living room.

"Mott, I'm home!"

"You're early," Mott called back from inside her room. Footsteps approached.

"Get under my bed," she whispered, yanking her blanket off her mattress.

Thrudi scooched under, and Mott handed her Fenris.

"Mott?" Her mother knocked lightly on the door.

"Just a minute!" Mott said, trying to not to sound like someone attempting to hide a Valkyrie and a moon-eating wolf under the bed. "I'm rearranging my room!"

Mott got on her hands and knees. "Are you okay under there? I know it's cramped. . . ."

"I am quite comfortable, provided I don't move."

"Good." Mott stuffed her blanket under her bed to keep Thrudi and Fenris out of view.

She opened her door.

"Were you talking to yourself?"

"Just practicing the script for my next root beer video." She smiled too much.

Her mom peered over her shoulder. "Putting your blanket under your bed is how you're rearranging your room?"

"It's a work in progress." Now she was smiling so much she could feel her mouth muscles straining. "Hey, Mom, why don't you change into dry clothes and then we can chat in the kitchen."

Why did Mott say "chat"? She never used the word "chat."

A few minutes later, they were in the kitchen, chatting. Mott only half listened while her mom got out pots and pans and ingredients to make soto ayam for dinner and explained why she was home early. It involved someone named Dolores and another person named Gloria and work shifts and doctor appointments and trading hours, and Mott just nodded along.

"How was your day?" Mom asked, chopping green onions.

Mott sat on a stool on the other side of the counter, mincing a shallot. She decided to give her mom an honest answer: "Today was really strange."

"Aw, I bet. Was it hard handing the pup over to the wolf rescue folks?"

"It was much harder than I thought."

"You did thing right thing, honey, and I'm proud of you."

Someone burped.

"Gross, Mott. What do you say?"

Fenris sat at Mott's feet, tail wagging. "Excuse me," she said, staring daggers into Fenris's soulful eyes.

Fenris released a mighty belch.

"Mott!"

"I'm thinking of changing my root beer ratings system from bubbles to burps. Belchenheim, two out of five burps." She fake-burped two times. Then Fenris burped, and Mott fake-burped again to cover Fenris's actual burp.

"Why don't you stick with bubbles?" her mom said. While she bent to grab another pan from the cupboard, Mott snatched up Fenris and rushed him back into her room.

"Sorry," Thrudi said in the open doorway. "He's slippery."

"Ungggh," Mott said, thrusting Fenris into her hands. "I have to help my mom make dinner or she'll get suspicious."

"I'll keep a tighter grasp on him," Thrudi said. "I promise."

"Are you talking to yourself again?" her mom called.

At a loss for what to say, Mott just burped and went back to the kitchen and started chopping cilantro.

"I spoke to your dad," Mott's mom said, keeping her tone casual, like this was something that happened every day.

"Oh, yeah?"

"He wanted to talk about sending you out to visit."

"Like I'm gonna fall for that one again."

"Mott . . ."

"It's fine," Mott said. "We practically just got to Culver City. I don't mind staying put. I haven't had much of a chance to get a feel for the place yet."

"But it's not fine. You know I don't like to talk trash about your dad. I want you to have a good relationship with him. You deserve to have a good relationship with him. But I hate that he breaks promises to you, and you need to know that it's not your fault."

Mott managed a smile. She hugged her mom around the waist. "Talking about feelings is gross."

Her mom kissed the top of her head. "It's not as gross as burping."

"Like this?" She let out an epic belch. Her mom tried not to laugh and failed.

"Well, maybe I'll get to see Dad before the end of the world," Mott said.

Her mom gave her a quizzical look, and they chopped vegetables together.

Hours later, after her mom had gone to bed, Mott slipped into her bedroom with a bowl of Indonesian chicken soup and a few bottles of root beer.

"You can come out," she whispered.

Thrudi and Fenris emerged from under the bed. Thrudi stretched her legs. "Oh, thank the All-Father."

"Sorry I left you stuck under there so long. My mom's not always home for dinner, so she wanted to talk. But I brought you some soto ayam."

Thrudi sat on Mott's bed and took in a whiff of the spicy noodles. She spent the next few minutes forking in mouthfuls.

"This is *so good*," she mumbled with a full mouth. "Better than cocoa. Dare I say, even better than root beer."

"Aw, yay," Mott said. "It's an Indonesian dish. My family's from Indonesia and Holland, mostly. Mom likes to make Indonesian food when she has time."

"She seems hardworking," Thrudi said.

"She is. She really tries to take care of us."

"You seem well capable of taking care of yourself," Thrudi said. That made Mott feel good. "Do you have more family?"

"Sort of." Mott showed Thrudi a picture on her phone. "This is my dad and his family. The blond woman is Carrie, his wife. My stepmom, I guess. The kids are Devin and Darla, my half siblings." They had Mott's dark skin, her brown eyes, her straight black hair. They looked so much like her, but she barely knew them. She sent them birthday cards every year, and one time, she sent a case of Gorbenheimer root beer. Carrie sent back a thank-you card and signed their names.

Mott pointed at the golden retriever who sat between Devin and Darla like another brother, a member of the family. "This is Butch. I've never met him, but he looks nice."

After some thought, Mott drew a second checkmark

next to "Men forget the bonds of kinship."

Thrudi gave her a sad nod. "I couldn't help but over-hear you and your mother talking about your father. I don't wish to insult him, but he dishonors himself by breaking his oaths."

Mott climbed up on the bed next to Thrudi. Fenris sat between them, accepting belly scritches. "What's your family like?"

"My family was slain when a band of giants burned down our village," Thrudi said plainly.

It took Mott a moment to find her breath. "That's horrible."

"It was. But it was a long time ago. Those who did it are bones and dust now, hopefully suffering in Helheim. It is better than they deserve."

Thrudi's voice trailed off, and Mott could tell her thoughts were far away. Mott left her alone with them for a while. Only when Thrudi blinked and came back to the present did Mott have another question for her.

"You said bones and dust. I thought you were about my age. How old are you?"

"I am about your age. But I'm also ancient. Time works differently on my world than it does on yours. Anyway,

I survived, and I was found by the Valkyrie chieftain Radgrid. She took me to Asgard to dwell with her sister shield-maidens, and they are my family now. We are not related by blood, but rather are bound by oath and love." Thrudi studied Mott's face. "You don't have anyone in your life like that?"

"It sounds like you're talking about friends. I have a few. Amanda's my best friend. We're bound by root beer. But she's half a world away. Out here, in Los Angeles, it's pretty much just me. You want to see the root beer video review channel I do with her?"

"I only understood 'root beer,' but yes, please."

Mott was surprised to see a new video posted by Amanda. She'd toured the Gashimmel root beer factory in Berlin. She'd filmed root beer being made in vats, and conveyor belts transporting thousands of five-bubble-rated root beer bottles. She'd interviewed factory workers and Gassy, the Gashimmel mascot, who was dressed in a whole root beer bottle costume. The video had gotten the most views of anything on the channel. The comments were all "Best video yet, Amanda" and "The other girl seems lost without you" and "You should go solo."

Amanda didn't mention Mott in the video at all.

If Mott hadn't already checked "Man forgets the bonds of kinship," twice she would have done so now.

"Wow," was all Mott could say.

Thrudi's eyes softened. "You have one friend here, Mott. And if you ever met my sisters, I would speak to them of your courage and determination. They would embrace you as one of us. You would be our sister."

A warmth rose from Mott's belly and climbed to her cheeks. She threw her arms around Thrudi's neck, and while Thrudi didn't exactly return the hug, she didn't fight it, either.

"Do you think we can do it?" Mott said, letting her go. "Can we save everyone without sacrificing Fenris?"

Thrudi didn't answer right away.

"I don't think so," she said at last. "My mother taught me about prophecies when I was very small. She said they're strong. Once you fire an arrow, you can't unfire it. It's already too late."

"So . . . inevitable?"

"I'm afraid so."

"Then why bother fighting? If things are going to happen the way they're supposed to happen, why even try?"

Thrudi gave her a smile. It was kind and knowing.

Big-sisterly, Mott decided. "Because of another thing my mother taught me: it's not your job to finish the work of perfecting the world, but neither can you stop trying."

Now it was Mott's turn to be quiet. She wasn't sure if Thrudi's words gave her hope or made her feel too small for the promise she'd taken on.

"In any event, I have an idea," Thrudi said. "In Iron-wood there dwells a giant who raises the wolves of Fenris's kin. If your magic can find her, tomorrow we're going to visit Fenris's mother."

11

IRONWOOD NURSERY WAS A PEACH-COLORED
stucco cottage on the corner of two busy streets. Tables out
in front bore rows of herb and vegetable seedlings in plastic
trays and sagging sprays of exhausted flowers.

The weather had turned hot and cracking dry. Mott felt
like she could spark a fire just by snapping her fingers.

"Doesn't it seem awfully convenient that we're finding
all these gods and whatever else we need on the Westside
of Los Angeles?" she asked. "You say Fenris's mom lives
in Ironwood, and here's Ironwood Nursery, less than two
miles from home."

"The World Tree has different roots, but all worlds are
connected," said Thrudi. "And now, at the end of things,

the tendrils are getting tangled."

"Conveniently tangled," Mott insisted.

"I concede your point. Maybe it's Fenris. He's a focal point of Ragnarok. Places and people and events are converging on him."

Fenris sniffed the dirt, his nose twitching. His tail wagged in an excited blur.

"Do you smell your mommy?" asked Mott.

"Mweep!" Nose to the ground, he followed a winding trail to the shop's front door. Mott kept close behind him.

Inside, the shop looked like most every other nursery Mott had been to. There was a counter and a cash register and sacks of potting soil, indoor plants hanging off hooks, racks of seeds in paper packets.

Nobody was there, but there was a back door. Maybe the nursery workers were outside. Fenris scratched the door with his front paws, and when Mott moved to open it, Thrudi put a hand on her shoulder.

"Mott," she said, "remember who we're looking for."

"Fenris's mom. So, a wolf."

"No, a giant. And she's not a friend, not to gods or humans. She's as dangerous in her own way as Tew or Vidar, and we are entering her realm."

"Okay, I'll be careful."

"Good. Does your magic device have any combat powers?"

"My phone? Not really."

"Then stay behind me." Thrudi limbered up, rolling her shoulders and touching her toes. She took the lead.

Behind the cottage, a warm wind howled through a small forest of potted palm trees. A distant boom echoed in the sky. Thunder? Crashing ocean waves?

"Can I help you find anything, girls?" A woman in a broad straw hat shoveled dirt into a clay pot. "We're running a sale on succulents."

"We seek the giant Angrboda," Thrudi said. "Does she dwell here?"

The woman smiled, deepening the wrinkles in the corners of her eyes. "Try over there," she said, pointing deeper into the nursery with her shovel.

Thrudi thanked her and went farther back in the yard.

Mott and Fenris followed, but before Mott slipped between rows of ornamental orange trees, she glanced back at the woman.

It seemed wrong that a nursery worker on Venice Boulevard would know a giant.

"How long has this nursery been here?"

The worker didn't answer. She just shoveled a little more dirt before heading into the cottage.

Mott watched her go. "You have your sword, right, Thrudi?"

"Always. Though for what we might be facing, I fear it's not much more than a security blanket."

"Oh, terrific," Mott muttered.

Fenris's nose twitched faster, and his tail wagged swifter, and before Mott could stop him, he yipped and surged ahead, out of sight, into a shadowed maze of trees.

When Mott and Thrudi caught up with him, he wasn't alone.

On the root of a gnarled tree sat a woman in a simple white gown. Her hair was ice-white and her skin so pale it was almost blue. A litter of wolf cubs squabbled at her feet, mixes of gray and white and black fur, all Fenris's size. They growled and whined, threatening as Mott and Thrudi approached. Fenris whimpered and turned over to expose his belly.

"I thought you'd be bigger," Mott blurted out.

"Mott . . . ," Thrudi warned.

Mott hadn't meant to be rude. She was just nervous.

"Bigger compared to what?"

"It's just . . . Thrudi said you were a giant, so . . ."

She rose to her feet, graceful as water. "That word does not mean the same thing in all lands. I am a Jotun, and my forms are without number. But as the worlds are splintering, as we swirl, wind-strewn on the edge of the storm, I can accommodate your expectations if it gives you comfort."

Mott didn't see her change. It wasn't like she stretched and grew taller. She was just so much larger now, her gaze cast down from a great height, her voice like a whisper from the clouds.

"I can grow larger still, if it suits you."

Her wolf pups yipped laughter.

Fenris shivered.

"No," Mott said hastily. "No, no, thank you."

"I have a question for you both," the giant said. "Why have you brought Fenris to me? Or, why have I been brought to Fenris?"

Mott decided to let Thrudi do the talking from now on.

Thrudi bowed in a way that looked like it was something she practiced. "Lady Angrboda, your child is in danger. Tew pursues him, and Vidar as well. We come seeking your help before Fenris is harmed, and before he harms the worlds."

"Well spoken, Valkyrie," Angrboda said. "But you haven't answered my question. Why have you brought Fenris to *me*?"

Now Thrudi faltered. "Because . . . you're his mother."

"I was, once. But that was long ago. He stopped being my child when Tew fed him the Annihilation Rune. All my children are mighty beasts, but no great threat to the worlds. Fenris is different. He is a destroyer now. I cannot help him. And I will not try."

Fenris took a step forward to join his littermates, but one harsh look from Angrboda sent him scurrying back to Mott.

"It's not his fault," Mott protested. "He didn't do this to himself. You should have protected him. You should protect him now. You should love your kids all the same."

"If only my children were all the same," the giant said.

She changed again, though it was hard to say exactly how. She didn't grow bigger; her color didn't shift, nor her shape and form. But she became somehow colder. Fog roiled off her white skin. Her every breath howled with Arctic wind. The air thickened, clouds of fog combining into a thick cottony wall.

"We have to go," Thrudi said urgently.

Mott bent down to gather Fenris, but she couldn't see him. Even her own hands disappeared in the swirling murk. "Fenris?"

Fenris's small whines sounded far away. Mott looked around desperately, calling for him, trying to spot him in the gloom.

"Thrudi, do you have him?"

"I can't see anything," came Thrudi's distant voice.

"I'm here," Mott called back. "Reach for me." Mott stretched out her hands, grasping nothing.

"Mott, where are you?" Thrudi continued calling out, but her voice grew thinner, less substantial, until it faded away entirely.

The only voices Mott heard now were her own, and then, one more time, the giant's. "Sometimes you have to make choices, girl," the giant said. "And when the world is cruel, so are the choices."

"Fenris?" Mott called. "Thrudi?"

There were no answers. Mott stumbled through the fog.

◆ ◆ ◆

Mott didn't know how long she'd wandered in the shrouded nursery. Long enough that her throat was raw from screaming out for Thrudi and Fenris.

She figured Thrudi could take care of herself, but what about the pup? The last thing he'd heard was his mother saying she didn't love him. That she wouldn't help him. He must be so scared. And so sad.

"Fenris?" she called again.

"There's no need to shout."

"Who's there? I can't see you." Whoever spoke, they sounded close. The voice was rich, chocolaty.

"The air is a bit whiffy, isn't it? Let's fix that."

Fog swirled away like water down a drain, forming a clearing. On a big, upturned flowerpot sat a man. Fenris snuggled in his lap.

"Don't you hurt him," Mott said.

"Why would I hurt my own child?"

His face was as pleasant as his voice, with gentle pale eyes and the graceful lines of his cheeks narrowing to lips poised in an amused smile. But Mott wasn't fooled. She knew who this was.

"If Fenris is your son, that means you're Loki."

"Ah, you've heard of me. How flattering."

"You're in the encyclopedia."

"Don't believe anything you read. Or that you're told. Or that you think. Honestly, just assume everything's a lie and you'll be okay." Light danced in Loki's eyes like a flickering flame. He laughed. It was an infectious laugh. It almost made Mott want to laugh along. She bit the insides of her cheeks.

"Hermod said you're a trickster, and a shape-changer, and a liar."

Loki pointed a long finger at her. "Okay, first of all, I didn't kill Baldr. They just like to blame me for every nasty thing that happens."

"Who's Baldr?"

"Killing Baldr was my most hilarious gag. It was the first step in Ragnarok. It's why the worlds are ending."

"You just said you *didn't* kill Baldr."

Loki put his hand over his mouth and made an exaggerated *oops* face. "You caught me. I better watch myself around you."

"If you're a shape-shifter, does that mean Fenris is, too?"

Fenris's belly gurgled.

"Well, something's shifting in there. How much has he

eaten while you were dog-sitting him?"

Mott shook her head. "I'm not listening to you. Please hand Fenris over."

"And then what? You let him eat us all up?"

"Maybe," Mott shot back.

Loki laughed. "Well, that's fine with me. Sometimes a world deserves to end."

Mott wouldn't let herself get drawn into some big argument about the fate of the universe. "You're an awful dad."

"Not the worst dad, though, am I?" He winked at her.

"How . . . how do you know about my dad?"

He laughed. This laugh was *not* infectious. This one was sharp enough to draw blood. "I don't. I was just guessing. But let's talk about your father, since you brought him up. Sort of absent from your life? Plays favorites with his other kids? Maybe . . . maybe makes promises he doesn't keep?"

"You're a good guesser," Mott said, her voice rigid.

"I'm sorry. Am I making you angry? Or am I just a convenient target for the anger you already harbor?"

Mott found herself shaking. Words got tangled in her throat. With just a few questions, Loki had managed to draw up all her sadness, her disappointment, all the cold, empty feelings of being forgotten. He'd done it so quickly and so efficiently, and not with lies, but with truths.

Mott closed her eyes and drew in a shuddering breath. *This isn't about me,* she thought to herself. *This is about Fenris. I'm not my father. I keep my promises.*

When she opened her eyes, she didn't say anything, but she let her face tell Loki that she wouldn't be distracted from her goal.

Loki stroked Fenris's fur. Fenris didn't seem to mind. "How about we make a deal? I'll give you the pup, but you have to take something else from me as well."

Bargaining with a trickster god was a bad idea. "What's the 'else'?"

"Only this." Like a magician conjuring a white dove into existence, he produced a stem with narrow green leaves and little white berries.

Mott squinted at it. "That's mistletoe. People kiss underneath it at Christmas."

"You know your plants. Very good. But mistletoe isn't just about smooching by the stockings. It has other properties as well." He turned the bouquet in his hands, examining it from all angles. "For one thing, it's a parasite. It feeds off trees, stealing their water and nutrients. Such a naughty shrub." He shook a finger at it. "But being a parasite isn't what makes mistletoe remarkable. It has other properties. There are beings among us so strong that they're almost impossible to harm, not by fire, not by water, not by steel or stone. But then, there's this." He held the mistletoe out to Mott, close enough for her to grab. "That's due to some clever magic that I had absolutely nothing to do with," he continued, lying extravagantly and not appearing to care if Mott knew it. "This modest little parasite . . . I call it the god-killer. You should take it."

He pushed the mistletoe closer to Mott's nose.

"What for?"

"Well, to kill the wolfling. What else?"

Mott ground her teeth together so hard her gums hurt. "You are the worst father in the nine worlds. You're right about my dad. He's broken every promise he ever made me. He sucks. But even he isn't telling anyone to kill me."

Loki seemed delighted. "As far as you know."

"I won't hurt Fenris. Ever."

"If that's true, then what's the harm in taking it?"

Loki continued to pet Fenris. The pup's eyes grew heavy. In a few more seconds, he was snoring.

"You *want* me to take it," Mott said. "That's reason enough not to."

"Even after all the mayhem he's already caused?"

"Tew force-fed him the Annihilation Rune. None of this is Fenris's fault."

"Is it your mother's fault, then?" Loki countered.

"What's my mom got to do with it?"

"She's part of the world, isn't she? She lives in it. She walks on it. She breathes and works and shops on it. So if the world ends, she dies. Is that what you want?"

"Of course not."

"Of course not," Loki agreed. "But you can save her, Mott. You can save everybody. All you have to do is take the mistletoe. Wrap it around that tiny pocketknife of yours. Cut open my son and take out the rune. Billions of lives saved, for the loss of one animal. Isn't that a small cost to protect your mother?"

"So . . . are you saying Ragnarok can be prevented? That it's not inevitable?"

"Who told you it's inevitable? A god? You believe everything gods tell you?"

"Is it, or isn't it?"

"There's really only one way to find out." He held out

the mistletoe so close that the berries touched Mott's nose.

She batted them away. "Please just give me Fenris back," Mott said.

"I'm afraid this is an all-or-nothing deal."

"Why are you like this?"

"Because I find it all deliciously funny. I'm sorry. I am what I am. I can be nothing else. But you can make a choice: The wolf, or your mother. Along with, you know, many billions of people."

"I choose the wolf," Mott said with a snarl.

Loki clicked his tongue. "I'm a lord of lies, Mott. You think I can't tell when someone's fibbing?"

Mott tried to hold his gaze. Her eyes felt hot just looking at him.

Loki took a thoughtful breath. "You know, it's better to have a sandwich when you're not hungry than to have no sandwich when you are."

"What's that supposed to mean?"

"Now you're lying again. You know what it means."

Mott did, but she wasn't going to give him the satisfaction of saying so. He meant it was better to have a way to kill Fenris that she would never use than a need to kill him but no way to do it.

But she wouldn't kill Fenris.

She'd promised to protect him.

She would never cut the rune from his belly.

Even if it meant the world would come to an end?

All the worlds?

And everyone would die?

Even her mom?

Mott snatched the mistletoe out of Loki's hand. Without looking at it, she wadded it up and stuffed it in her pocket.

Loki released Fenris. Mott gathered him in her arms and held him tight.

Loki giggled.

Then he chortled.

He guffawed.

He cackled.

He howled and shrieked into the echoing sky and pigeons burst from the trees and glass broke and ashes shook loose from the clouds.

Thrudi's voice rang out in the fog. "Mott? Mott, can you hear me?"

"I'm right here! I have Fenris! Follow my voice!"

But it turned out there was no need for that. The air thinned, and the tables of potted plants and the trays of vegetable seedlings and the wheelbarrows and shovels reappeared. The heat returned, the air so dry Mott's tongue felt like wood.

The nursery worker in the straw hat went about her work as if nothing had ever changed, as if moments ago the world hadn't been blanketed by fog, as if this wasn't a place where Mott had stood before giants.

Loki was gone.

Thrudi clapped Mott on the back. "You're still alive! Well done!"

"It was just some fog," Mott said.

"It was a magic fog, probably summoned to conceal lies and misdeeds. I'm glad you're unharmed. And you found Fenris." Thrudi's cheer dimmed when she seemed to notice Mott's mood didn't match her own. "What's wrong?"

"I met Loki," Mott admitted.

And now Thrudi's demeanor became grave. "Tell me everything."

Mott told her everything. Except about the mistletoe.

She never should have accepted it from Loki.

She should toss it to the ground right now.

She should stomp it, drive it into the dirt.

But it stayed in her pocket, tucked tight against her knife.

12

THE FULL MOON HOVERED LOW in the crisp blue sky, so big and clear that Mott could count every crater. Outside the nursery, the air was pizza-oven hot.

"We should check for Tew's whereabouts," Thrudi said.

"No new sightings on NeighborSnoop," Mott reported after a few minutes on her phone. "But the intersection where Tew and Vidar fought is rubble now."

"I'm sure Tew is delighted." Thrudi got out her sword and scraped the blade with a sharpening stone. "Wide-spread destruction and death will be his contribution to Ragnarok. And if he gets his hands on . . ."

She didn't finish the sentence. She didn't need to. Fenris mweeped and curled up in Scooty's basket.

On an impulse, Mott got out her phone and checked the

weather in Pennsylvania. They were having a winter storm in June. High winds. Hail. Ice. She watched her thumbs type out a text to her dad: "Are you safe?"

The only thing worse than finding out her dad and stepmom and brother and sister were in danger would be her dad answering with no more than a terse word or two. Or not bothering to answer at all. She sent the text anyway and tried to forget about it.

When she put the phone back in her pocket, her fingers brushed against the mistletoe. She suppressed a shiver. Loki had given her the god-killing herb for a reason.

"Thrudi, you broke a promise once, didn't you?" After spending time with her and seeing the way Fenris acted around her, Mott knew Thrudi hadn't told her everything about Fenris's escape.

Thrudi took her time before answering. "I told you that where I come from, an oath-breaker is one of the worst things one can be. When you break an oath, you prove you have no loyalty. You show that you're a liar. That you're weak. And I did break my promise to stand guard over Fenris. I am an oath-breaker." She looked up at the daytime moon. "I freed Fenris. And I would do it again."

"Why?"

"Because he was suffering. He was being punished for something he hadn't yet done."

"But didn't the prophecy say he would?"

"If the prophecy is true, Fenris will destroy the worlds regardless of what I did. At least this way, I'm not guilty of cruelty. So if I broke my promise, if I'm an oath-breaker, I guess I'm not sorry."

Mott followed Thrudi's gaze to the moon. "I think I might have to make a choice," she said, more to herself than to Thrudi.

"Each moment is a choice." An old man on the corner came their way. "But we don't always get to be the ones making it."

Mott hadn't noticed him before: hunched shoulders, ratty gray sweater, one clear eye, one eye hidden in a squint.

"I know you," she said.

"That's right. You bought me a scoop of root beer ice cream. It was delicious."

"And now you're suddenly here, miles from the ice cream shop. This is not a coincidence."

Fenris hid farther in the basket.

Thrudi ran her stone down her blade with a sharp scrape and a hard stare.

"You're right, Mott," the man said. "There is no such thing as coincidence. No such thing as a random encounter. Everything has been predicted. Seen. Contemplated."

Two huge crows dove from the sky, each landing on one of the old man's shoulders. Their claws gleamed like black glass. Light glinted off their black feathers.

"I've seen these crows," Mott said, enduring their penetrating gazes. "They were there when Fenris ate Gorm the Vicious."

Thrudi dropped her sharpening stone. "Those aren't crows," she said, trying to control her breathing. "They are the ravens Huginn, Thought, and Muninn, Memory. That means you are . . ."

The old man lifted his chin. He straightened his back and shoulders. "Yes," he said.

Thrudi dipped her head in a bow. "Forgive me, Odin All-Father. I didn't recognize you."

"Well, why would you?" He winked his clear eye. "I'm in disguise! Pretty good, huh?" He turned to Mott. "I have a habit of roaming the earth, pretending to be penniless and frail, asking for a roof over my head, a place near a warm fire, some bread, some ale, maybe even meat. Most places turn me away. But every now and then I find a kind host. Someone who treats me like a king, though I look like a pauper. They offer hospitality when they think they have nothing to gain from it, simply being kind for the sake of kindness. If I go around looking like myself . . ." And for just an instant, he was tall, broad-shouldered, his face framed by an elaborately braided beard, armored in sun-bright gold, his squinty eye open to a deep black chasm that rivaled Fenris's yawn, and Mott had to put her hand on Scooty's saddle to steady herself. ". . . then people are going to be nice to me because I'm king of the gods."

To Mott's relief he returned to his humbler appearance.

"So it's a test," she said.

"If they're kind, they see good fortune. Silver and gold. Bountiful crops, plump babies. Stuff like that."

"But if they're not?" Mott said, nervous about how he judged their encounter at the ice cream shop.

"Then they get barren fields, a spear through the skull on the battlefield, constant toothaches."

"Um . . . how did I do?

"You did splendidly. You defended me to that mean kid with the scooper. And you forwent your own elaborate treat to buy me a cone. You shared. You were hospitable. I don't see as much of that as I used to. And you have earned a reward."

Please no plump babies, please no plump babies, thought Mott.

He reached an age-spotted hand in the pocket of his loose pants and produced a milky white sphere about the size of a ping-pong ball.

"Sometimes, Mott, we are offered only that which is awful." Mott thought about the mistletoe in her own pocket. "But sometimes we receive something wonderful."

He held the sphere out to her and placed it in her palm. It was hard, like stone, and heavy.

"What is it?"

Odin grinned, proud. "It's my eye!"

"Gah!" Mott said without thinking.

Thrudi was excited. "Your eye? The one you plucked from your own face and cast into Mimir's well in exchange for wisdom?"

"The very one, but I didn't think I got much wisdom for it, so I took it back. A refund, sort of."

"Thank you," Mott said, trying not to think about all the places it had been, especially not Odin's eye socket. "Will this help us save Fenris? And the nine realms?"

Odin shrugged one shoulder. "I doubt it. I've spent my life trying to avert the events of Ragnarok, yet look around us. Here we are. But your kindness and courage have given me hope. Not a lot of it. But a little light and warmth in this storm. Perhaps, just perhaps, my eye can give you some light in return."

He stepped over to Fenris and gave him a scritch behind the ear. Fenris cowered. "Don't worry, wolfling. I know you have to devour me. We all must play our part. I won't take it personally. And now I'm off."

"Odin . . . All-Father," Thrudi said, "won't you help us?"

"No. I want to enjoy my last hours before the universe dies. Try some things I've never gotten around to. You know I've never ridden a roller coaster? Or had a corn dog on a stick? Good luck saving the worlds, girls. This god is busy."

Exactly like an old man heading to enjoy his afternoon, Odin walked down the sidewalk, around the corner, and was gone.

Mott stared at the eye. "I get that this is a big, important gift from a big, important god, but it's also an eyeball, which makes it gross, so I'm just going to put it in my pocket now."

"A very Midgardian reaction, but I understand."

Mott's phone trilled. She frowned. "It's my mom." Mom never called during work, only texted. "Mom, is everything okay?" she answered.

"Mott!" came her mom's frantic voice. "Please tell me you're home."

Thrudi mimed drowning in a creek.

There were sounds in the background. People screaming. Somebody or something went "Baawwww."

"Mom, what's going on? Where are you?"

"I'm at the museum, the catering job, and . . . I don't know. Things are weird."

"What do you mean 'weird'?"

"AAGUH, GET AWAY FROM ME!" screamed Mott's mom.

"Mom, what's happening? Are you being attacked by someone in leathers and animal furs who is also carrying a sword or a huge ax?"

"No," her mom said. "That was very specific."

"Glub, glub, drowning," Thrudi said.

Mott ignored her. "Mom, tell me what's going on."

"Shoo!" her mom said. "Yuck!"

"Mom?"

"Mott, just stay home and lock the doors. And stay away from cemeteries."

"Why would I be hanging around cemeteries?"

Her mom didn't say anything back.

"Mom?"

Nothing.

"MOM!"

And still, nothing. Her mom had hung up.

13

THE ART MUSEUM OCCUPIED AN entire block on a big, busy street called the Miracle Mile, and it was a miracle that Mott and Thrudi arrived in one piece. The traffic lights were out, and people were driving like they were in a game and hitting a scooter would earn them points. The air smelled of smoke. The sky had turned orange.

On the plaza in front of the museum entrance, cops tried to clear people out of the area, but not in any organized way. They screamed at terrified museum visitors, and the terrified museum visitors screamed back. It was a chaotic clog.

Fenris watched all this with bright-eyed interest, blepping his tongue.

Mott pushed her way into the crowd. Through the museum's big front windows, she could see something moving across the lobby. It was human-shaped, thin, draped in torn rags.

The huge sign over the doors gave her a strong clue of what it was:

Treasures of the Ancients

Special Exhibit, Limited Time Only, Ticket Required

Featuring King Tut and Additional Mummies!

"I'm going in," she told Thrudi.

Thrudi drew her sword. "I figured."

Mott wished Odin had given her a sword instead of an eyeball. Even a stick would be more useful for batting away mummies. "I don't suppose you have any more weapons in your bag? In case I need to get into some action?"

"In the right hands, anything's a weapon, Mott."

"So, that's a no?"

Thrudi rummaged in her bag. She handed Mott a bottle of root beer.

"What am I supposed to do with this?"

"Stay hydrated."

With all the running and screaming and fear and noise in the plaza, nobody seemed to notice a girl with a sword and another girl cradling a wolf pup slip into the museum.

Some small part of Mott had believed that she would charge inside, find her mom, get her someplace safe, and all this stuff involving Fenris and gods and the end of the world would sort itself out. But instead of her mom's face, what she saw was leathery skin stretched over a skull, and long, skeletal arms swaddled in broad ribbons of decaying woven fabric. It was one of those "additional mummies."

"Muurrrrgh," said the mummy, stumbling toward her with twiggy fingers. Its papery skin crackled when it moved.

"This is really not how I thought this day was going to go," said Mott.

Fortunately, the mummy was the slow kind of walking dead, and Mott and Thrudi left it shambling in the lobby.

"My mom works in the kitchens. I think they're this way."

They sprinted down corridors and through several galleries where the floors were littered with museum brochures and dropped phones and even a few paintings knocked off the walls.

"Don't you nibble that painting!" Mott ordered Fenris,

who was taking an experimental sniff of a Picasso.

He narrowed his eyes at Mott and pulled his lips back to show teeth. A wisp of dust rose from the floor, swirled around his mouth. It made Mott think of stars falling into a black hole.

"Fenris, no," Mott said firmly.

Fenris growled, sounding bigger than he was. Something was changing. Fenris was changing. For the first time, he was frightening. After a few seconds, he returned to his usual demeanor and gave her an apologetic mweep. He let her pick him up.

They turned a corner and came face-to-face with another beef-jerky-fleshed mummy. "Uuurrrrgh," it said, clacking its teeth.

Mott recognized this one. His withered face was on the signs in front of the museum.

This was no "additional mummy."

This was Tutankhamen himself.

King Tut.

Thrudi brandished her sword. "Stand back!"

But before Thrudi could attack, Mott hurled a Borbles root beer bottle at the ancient walking dead pharaoh / global tourist attraction. Glass shattered. Root beer foamed.

"Baaawww," moaned the mummy, retreating.

As a weapon, Mott rated Borbles five out of five bubbles.

"I am so happy I devoted my life to root beer," she exulted.

But while she was congratulating herself, she lost her grip on Fenris.

Fenris, nose-twitching.

Fenris, tail-wagging.

Fenris, tongue-blepping.

Fenris, containing the Annihilation Rune.

Mott knew exactly what was going to happen. She would try to stop Fenris, and she would fail, because that's how the whole Ragnarok prophecy was designed.

"No, puppy, no!" she shouted, as if reading a script.

And, of course, Fenris ignored her.

He widened his maw into an all-consuming tunnel. The world went sideways and weird. Debris skittered across the floor, drawn by Fenris's gravitational force. Wind howled. The mummy fluttered his hands, and his feet left the floor as he was swept toward the chasm inside Fenris.

In an instant, Tutankhamen was gone, and Fenris sat, eyes bright, licking flecks of ancient bandage wraps from his fuzzy muzzle.

"You just ate King Tut!" Mott screamed. "You can't eat King Tut! You ate him!"

"Mweep."

"Who's King Tut?" Thrudi clearly failed to understand the magnitude of what had happened.

"He's only the most famous mummy of all time!"

Thrudi stared blankly. "He's famous for being dead and well preserved?"

Mott rubbed her eyes in frustration. "Let's keep looking for my mom."

In the cafeteria, tipped-over chairs lay amid spilled sandwiches and salads and beverages. Entire meals sat abandoned on tables. But it was the absence of people that hollowed out Mott's chest. Where was her mom?

Calling out, she rushed around the dining room, checking under tables. She looked behind the counters, pushed through the double doors to the kitchen, checked a supply room.

"I'm sure she got out safely," Thrudi said. "We just missed her in the chaos. Come, we'll go outside and find her."

"I don't think so," Mott said. "I think we're just going to keep failing at everything we try."

"That's fear talking." Thrudi put a hand on her shoulder. "Don't give into it."

"It's just going to get worse and worse, isn't it? The weather, the rising dead, my mom going missing. I never used to think about the end of the world. It was something in the far future that happened to other people. But look at this." She gestured at the abandoned cafeteria. "And it's my fault."

"How is it your fault?"

Mott's hand went into her pocket. Her fingers brushed against her pocketknife and the mistletoe she'd accepted from Loki.

Fenris took a pause from lapping up cheesecake on the ground and focused his trusting eyes on her.

Mott jerked her hand out of her pocket. "I just shouldn't have let any of this happen."

"You're right," said Hermod. "This is your fault."

Where before there had been an unoccupied table, Hermod the messenger god now sat, gazing deep into a paper cup of coffee. The shadows in his gaunt face were even deeper than when Mott and Thrudi had visited his house. He took a sip from his cup. "You could have just turned the animal over to Tew or Vidar. You could have gone home to spend the world's last sunset with your mother."

Thrudi grunted. "Speak your message and say no more, messenger."

Hermod looked to the ceiling. He looked to the walls. Finally, reluctantly, he looked at Mott with haunted eyes.

"I know where your mother is," he said. "She's in Helheim."

14

IT SNOWED ASHES IN LOS Angeles.

Mott watched deep orange flames spread over the Hollywood hills like lava, consuming brush and houses. Every one of those houses was home to a person, a family, someone with old photo albums and a grandmother's handwritten recipes on index cards. Every lost house belonged to someone with pets. Someone with a life.

Haze turned the afternoon sunlight to an eerie red. Helicopters braved the smoke, disappearing into a wall of black clouds. But even through the smoke, the moon shone, an amber disc the size of a pancake.

Mott dragged out her root beer journal. She'd already checked off "Surtur, flame-wielding, sets the land on fire."

That left only two items unchecked:

- The wolf Fenris swallows the moon and sun.
- An age of axes. An age of swords. And an age of wolves, till the world goes down.

Fenris lifted his head to the sky. "Aroo," he said in an attempted howl.

Mott petted his shoulders. "Shhh, puppy, it's okay. It's going to be okay."

It had to be okay.

Fenris had to be okay.

Mott's mom had to be okay.

Mott had to make it okay before it was too late.

If it wasn't too late already.

Hermod had led Mott and Thrudi and Fenris to the Grove, an outdoor shopping center near the art museum.

"You said you know where my mother is." Grit coated the back of Mott's throat. Her lungs burned.

Hermod spread his arms in a grand gesture. "She's here. In Helheim."

Despite the grainy air, people went in and out of stores. They carried bags. They pushed strollers. They looked at their phones. They rubbed red eyes and brushed ash off their clothes. They ate frozen yogurt and coughed in the smoke. The world was burning around them, and they shopped.

"This isn't Helheim," Thrudi scoffed. "This is a marketplace."

Mott picked a flake of ash out of Fenris's white fur. "We call it a shopping mall. I thought Helheim was the land of the dead."

Hermod cleared his throat. "Maybe we disagree on the definition of living."

Thrudi gave up all show of bowing and politeness and manners. "If we wanted riddles, we'd go to Loki."

A man emerged from a shoe shop with a box of new shoes and a hacking cough. He dusted ash out of his hair and retreated from the smoke into an eyeglass store.

"Helheim is a place of hopelessness," Hermod said. "Do you see hope here? All I see is habit. Shopping. Accumulating. These people are raking fields where crops will never grow. They're plucking twigs instead of fruit. They're—"

"Where is my mom?" Mott snapped, her throat raw with smoke. She had no more patience for talk. She'd faced Vidar and Tew and Fenris's parents. She'd chased a dead man's hand and been chased by walking mummies. All of it was weird and frightening. But those were her choices. Her mom hadn't asked for any of this.

"I'm here, Mott."

Mott spun around.

Her mother's face was drawn with stress. A deep frown creased her forehead, but Mott didn't see any wounds or injuries.

"Are you okay, honey?"

"I'm okay, Mom."

Behind her mother, not touching her but close enough if he wanted to, was Vidar.

Mott reached out her hand. "Come here, Mom."

The lines in her mother's face grew even deeper. "I can't. I can't move. This man . . . he's done something to me."

"Magic," Thrudi said.

Mott gritted her teeth. "You let her go, Vidar. Right now, or I'll . . ."

Vidar shook his head, just slightly, a little sadly. "I admire your courage. On another day, I would gladly fight beside you. But this is no ordinary day. I have a task. And you, Mott, have a choice. You can agree to a trade. You can give me the beast and spend the world's last moments in the comfort and care of your mother. Or you can delay me from serving my function. If that is your choice, I will still tear the beast asunder, and your mother will suffer."

"I don't understand any of this." Her mom's voice shook. "I don't know who any of these people are or what's going on. But I want you to walk away right now, Mott. It'll be fine. I'll be okay."

Mott was only dimly aware of everything around her. The sky was red, the moon looming. There were people gawking. Some snapping pictures or video with their phones. Some choking in the thickening smoke. And others continuing to shop at the end of the world.

Somebody large moved in Mott's peripheral vision: Tew. The war god's ax was slung over his shoulder. He slurped an iced mocha through a straw.

"I warn you, Tew . . . ," Vidar began.

"No, no, don't worry about me. I'm going to wait to see how this conflict plays out. Then, after that, you and I can settle our differences." He took another slurp.

Thrudi drew her sword. The crowd went "Oooooh."

Vidar closed his eyes. "I have always respected the Valkyries, and I would take no pride in killing you."

"I'm already in Helheim, and the day runs short," Thrudi said. "What does it matter if I'm alive or dead?"

Tew took yet another slurp of his mocha.

"Hey, guys, c'mon, why don't you let the girl's mother go," Hermod said, raising his hands in a peacemaking gesture. "If the prophecy is true, things will happen the way they're supposed to. No need to be big jerks about it."

"You have already performed your role, messenger," Vidar answered. "You may leave now if you wish. You must have precious time to waste elsewhere."

Fenris thumped his little tail against the pavement, splintering the concrete below his feet like a taco shell. He opened his mouth, and the air pressure dropped so quickly Mott's ears popped. Mott wasn't the only one who felt it. Everyone—Mott's mom, Thrudi, the gods—winced.

Black sludge fell from the sky and plopped to Earth, rain mixed with soot, and lightning flashed behind the smoke clouds.

Fenris stretched his jaws wide. He was a wolf-shaped creature. He was the offspring of shape-changing giants. He was a puppy. And he was a monster, a mountain of deep black shadow, eyes burning like magma, jagged lightning playing in teeth the size of icebergs. When he moved, ashes avalanched down his body.

He released a howl, the sound of the earth screaming in pain. The moon hung in the sky, defenseless as a wounded animal with nowhere to hide stalked by a predator.

Fenris the pup curled up against Mott's leg, whimpering.

Fenris the giant raked his teeth on the moon's surface.

He was both things at once, a creature that defied the reality of earthly rules.

Bone-cracking thunder drove Mott to her knees, but she forced herself to look at the sky. Glittering crumbs surrounded the moon like a halo. As seconds ticked, they grew brighter and bigger.

A horrified hush took the crowd. There were only a few voices. Some tried to reach loved ones over the phone. Some prayed. Some cried. But mostly Mott heard the strained silence of held breath.

Flaming streaks drew scars in the sky as moon fragments plummeted to Earth.

Mott felt as though she was standing on the edge of a crumbling cliff. And not just her alone, but everyone who played a part in this drama, everyone watching, everyone in the mall, and everyone in the world.

Mott didn't know what her role was, but she had to do something. She didn't have a sword. But she did have a weapon. She reached into her pocket.

"Thrudi," she said softly, to get the Valkyrie's attention. Thrudi saw what Mott held in her hand.

"You have mistletoe?"

"Loki gave it to me. I should have told you. I'm sorry."

Thrudi shook her head, dismissing Mott's apology. "You have a knife and the god-killing plant. You can use it to—"

"I know. I can cut Fenris open and remove the rune. Or let him eat the moon and sun and kill the worlds."

"Oh, my shield-sister," said Thrudi. "I am so sorry you've been burdened with this poisonous choice. You know that I'll stand with you no matter what you decide. But you must choose."

Mott wanted to hug Thrudi and squeeze her tight. Ragnarok was no longer something that might happen. Not even something that *would* happen. It was happening right now.

Tew shook his mocha and enjoyed another slurp. "I don't know how many times you need to be told the way the prophecy works, girl. Try anything you like, and you will fail. Ragnarok will happen, because it must. Fenris will eat the moon, because he must. Vidar will kill Fenris, because he must. And the nine worlds will end. Because . . .

I think you get it by now. You're just drawing things out."

Mott pressed the mistletoe into Thrudi's hand. "Take it," she said. "Hold them off as long as you can."

Thrudi entwined the strands of mistletoe around her blade. "And what are you going to do?"

Mott looked into her mom's dismayed and frightened eyes. "I'm going to save Fenris. And I'm going to save my mom. And I'm going to save my world, and all the others." Tears rose to her eyes. She gritted her teeth. "I promise."

Thrudi put her hand on Mott's shoulder. With a proud smile and tears of her own, she said, "I do not know how you're going to achieve the impossible, friend Mott. But I pledge my life to helping you try."

She raised her sword.

Tew snorted. "The prophecy says nothing about a Valkyrie besting any gods in combat. It says nothing about you at all, corpse-picker."

Thrudi smiled at the war god. "Good. That means you have no idea what I'll do before the end."

Vidar closed his eyes. "You will die along with all else."

"Maybe. But first I can make you bleed."

The longer Mott hesitated, the less likely she would have the courage to act.

She focused all her attention on Fenris. She ignored the shuddering Earth, the impact of moon crumbs, the smoke and flames, the impending battle between her friend and the mighty gods. She ignored her mother's pleas to just run away and leave her and everything else behind.

Only Fenris and Mott.

She took off her belt.

Made a loop at the end to form a leash.

Gripped it tight.

She bent down and started putting the loop around Fenris's head.

Just as she hoped, Fenris ate her.

15

MOTT HAD FALLEN BEFORE.

Every kid falls when they're taking their first steps. They fall when they're learning to ride a bike.

On Christmas when she was four, she'd gotten tired of listening to her parents argue instead of putting the star on top of the tree, so when nobody was watching, she climbed the ladder rung by rung with her short legs, all the way to the last one. When she saw how high she was, she panicked and lost her balance and tumbled from a height greater than she was tall. She'd suffered a knocked-out tooth and a sore elbow. The tooth would have fallen out in a couple of years anyway, her dad told her.

But that wasn't a real fall. Not like this.

Wind tore at her face, blinding her with tears, stripping off atoms the way Fenris stripped crumbs from the moon's surface. Her own screams sounded like an ambulance siren, and after a while, she was sure she was dead, and that death meant falling forever.

Maybe she'd lose consciousness at some point. She desperately hoped so.

But eventually, she stopped falling.

She didn't land, just stopped, feet on the ground, in total darkness.

She remembered the sign on the animal shelter's wall: *Inside of a dog, it's too dark to read.*

"Fenris?" she called.

Nothing.

"Hello?"

Still nothing. Not even an echo. She could barely hear herself. The nothingness swallowed her voice.

She put a hand in front of her face, hoping her eyes would adjust, but moments later, she still couldn't see anything. Nothingness wasn't a physical object—it was the absence of something—but she could feel it tugging at her, pulling her in every direction at once, slowly but steadily tearing her apart.

"Fenris, can you hear me?" she cried, desperate. She had never felt this alone. She'd never felt this far from her mother. From a friend, like Amanda, or from Thrudi's presence, strong and steady as iron. And her father felt as far away as ever.

The nothingness was swallowing *her*, and with it, her courage and her hope.

She took a tentative step but couldn't bring herself to take another. She could be on the edge of a cliff, or inches away from a curtain of webs crawling with spiders.

Maybe inside Fenris was her own personal Helheim, and here she would spend the rest of her life, the rest of the universe's life, shuffling in the dark.

"No," said Mott. It didn't matter that no one could hear her. It didn't matter that she was in Helheim. She would fight against the night until she won or until she couldn't fight anymore.

She recalled Odin's words: *Your kindness and courage have given me hope. . . . Perhaps my eye can give you some light in return.*

A light flickered in the corner of her eye. Her pocket was glowing, the one that contained Odin's eye. She reached for it, removed it from her pocket, held it high.

In the white glow, she could make out piles of rubble: jumbles of shattered concrete slabs with twisted steel bars growing out of them like weeds; splintered wood; some recognizable objects, like office furniture, charred refrigerators; wrecked cars, dented and burned, surrounded by broken glass. It went on for miles.

Inside Fenris was a world destroyed.

"Fenris?" she called again.

"Over here!"

In the distance, sitting atop a mound of debris, a man waved his arms.

"Climb up here with me," he said. "There's a monster around."

He was handsome and bearded and dressed in fur and armor, and Mott would have recognized him even if she'd never seen him in person before. It was Chris Hevans, the movie star.

"I'm strong and I can protect you." He flexed his arm and forced a grin. There was trauma in his bloodshot eyes. "That's a superhero bicep right there. It took a lot of work. Personal trainer, special diet . . ."

Mott had to admit that his biceps were magnificent.

She picked her way over. "Have you seen the wolf?"

"The one who ate me? We're inside of him, right? He's all around us?"

"Yeah."

"Nah, haven't seen him."

"Then what monster are you talking about?"

"There!" cried Chris Hevans. "It's right there!"

Something skittered at Mott's feet, and her heart thumped so hard she could taste it, but then she recognized the "monster." It looked like a spider made of rawhide.

"Oh, that," she said. "It's just a dead man's hand. It's harmless."

Chris Hevans wibbled. He flexed his other arm, as if his muscles gave him comfort.

"I can't stay here," Mott told him. "I'm looking for the Rune of Annihilation. I figure if I can destroy it, Fenris will stop trying to eat the moon and destroy the worlds. You want to help me look?"

Chris Hevans watched the hand scuttle back into the rubble. He wore the face of someone who'd just accidentally swallowed a bug. Gingerly, he climbed down the hill of wreckage.

"Good luck finding anything in all this mess. How big is the rune?" said a familiar voice.

Mott aimed Odin's light in its direction. Another man, also in furs and leather, idly spun the creaking wheel of an upturned bicycle. Mott recognized him, too:

Gorm the Vicious, Tew's minion.

"You're the one who nabbed Fenris after he ran away from the animal shelter," she said. "I looked away and, poof, you were gone."

"It wasn't a 'poof.' It was more of a 'munch, munch, swallow.'"

"Serves you right," Mott said. "You couldn't pay me a billion dollars to work for Tew."

"I didn't do it for money," Gorm said, his feelings hurt. "Tew pays in meat." He turned to Chris Hevans. "I'm Gorm."

Chis Hevans smiled with perfect teeth. "I'm Chris Hevans," said Chris Hevans. "I love your costume. Is that real fur?"

"No, it's—"

"Artificial?"

"—made from a troll's eyebrow."

"Oh," said Chris Hevans.

Mott resumed walking. "I'm going to keep looking for the rune."

"It's that way." Gorm pointed ahead toward a glimmer emerging from below the horizon, like a red sun that was neither rising nor setting.

"Then that's where I'm headed." Mott set off, trudging over the littered ground.

"Can I come with you?" Chris Hevans asked. "I don't want to be alone with that dead man's hand crawling around."

"If you want." Mott really didn't mind the company. She just wished Thrudi were here with her, because for all the awful, weird, scary things Mott had faced in the last couple of days, Thrudi had stood by her side. And being within the wrecked world inside Fenris was the awfullest, weirdest, scariest thing she'd done yet. But Thrudi was outside, fighting off gods to give Mott time to find the rune. She hoped she'd get to see her again.

Gorm raised his hand. "Um? Can I come, too? I think if I had company, I might not want to scream and sob."

"Yes, you, too," Mott said. "Just . . . don't get in my way and don't do anything mean or bad."

They trudged after her, following her light.

The closer they got to the source of the glow, the worse the devastation around them became. Mott saw things she wished she hadn't.

She saw bones—human bones—poking out of the clutter.

Random items had been dropped or lost in the ruins: sunglasses, shoes, phones, a wallet open to a picture of a smiling family of a mom and a dad and two girls and a boy. And a charred teddy bear, which was somehow the worst sight of all.

A woman with short silver hair and wire-rim glasses picked through rocks. One of her lenses was cracked. Her eyes were open too wide, like her face had frozen in an expression of fear.

"Bev? From the wolf rescue?"

"That's right." She lifted a rock, examined what was beneath it, and sighed. "Do you have any food? I haven't eaten proper since I left Idaho."

Mott regretted leaving all her root beer with Thrudi. "I don't. I'm sorry."

"Oh. Okay." Her voice was flat, emotionless, as if whatever she was feeling couldn't be fully expressed.

"I like meat," said Gorm.

Mott took the rock out of Bev's hands and put it down. "You should come with us."

"What about the wolf pup? Do you know where he is? I don't want to see him again."

Fenris was all around them. Fenris was everywhere.

"He's nearby," Mott said. "But if you stay brave, I can help get you out of here."

Bev moved her head. It was less a headshake than a shudder. "I don't know. . . ."

Mott offered Bev her hand. "Take it. It'll be okay."

Bev hesitated. "You promise?"

Mott almost said yes. But it would be lying. "I honestly don't know how this is going to end. We just have to keep trying and hope for the best."

"Thank you for being honest," Bev said. She accepted Mott's hand.

The party moved on toward the red glow. Even the dead man's hand followed along, darting in and out of cover.

Mott lost track of time. Had she been inside Fenris for minutes, hours, or days? Her head said minutes, but her tired bones said centuries.

She pushed through the fatigue, one step at a time, one foot after the other, relentless, until finally she found the source of the glow. The light seeped through a field of rocks and charred earth like blood through a bandage. Mott found the brightest spot and fell to her knees. She started digging with her fingers.

Bev knelt beside her to help.

Chris Hevans grabbed handfuls of dirt.

Gorm joined them.

Even the dead man's hand pitched in, scraping the ground with its fingernails.

After a time, they uncovered something. Mott moved Odin's eye closer to get a good look. It was a thin rectangle the size of a domino, black as coal except for a design: an eight on its side, the symbol for infinity, with a slash through it, glowing red like steel in a blacksmith's forge.

Gorm stood and stepped back. "The Annihilation Rune," he said. Fear put a quaver in his voice.

Mott reached for it.

"Careful!" warned Bev. "It'll burn you."

"No," Gorm said. "When it's whole, it contains its heat within. But crack it open, and the devastation will be instant."

"Like an atom?" Mott asked.

"Yes," said Gorm. He paused. "Actually, I have no idea what an atom is."

"I know what an atom is," Chris Hevans announced, proudly puffing his chest. "I defused a nuclear missile when I played special agent Jason Mussel in a little film you may have heard of called *Jason Mussel, Special Agent*."

Mott also knew about atoms. They were the building blocks of elements. Every object in the universe was made of them. But if you split an atom apart it released an unbelievable amount of energy. If you split enough atoms apart, you could power an entire city. Or destroy one.

Mott picked up the rune. Even though it wasn't hot, Mott sensed its danger, as if she was holding a ticking bomb.

"Puppy?" Mott called out. "Can you hear me? I know you're out there. I found the thing that Tew forced down your throat. If you'll let me help, I can take it away from you."

Was there an answer? Maybe there was a change in the background noise. Maybe an increase in the wind, like a breath. Maybe a deep, pulsing thump. Or maybe it was Mott's own heartbeat.

"It's up to you, puppy," Mott said to the sky. "You don't have to be a destroyer if you don't want to be. Just like you don't have to let some old prophecy tell you what you are. You can barf the rune out, and us with it. But I can't make you. It's up to you."

This was the extent of Mott's plan. The universe had made a promise. Mott had made a promise. She didn't know if Fenris had ever made a promise. Despite everything that made him powerful and strange, he was still an animal, and she didn't know if an animal *could* make a promise.

But maybe he could make a choice.

Now there definitely was a noise.

There was a gurgle.

A slosh.

A roar, rising in intensity.

Rubble clacked and shifted. Pebbles streamed down the hills of wreckage. The ground beneath Mott's feet trembled, and the world inside Fenris filled with the din of crashing boulders and screaming glass.

Something big was coming.

A tidal wave?

No. It was a lot grosser than that.

Mott clutched the rune tight.

16

MOTT LAY FACEDOWN, SPRAWLED ON the plaza of the Grove mall.

"Ew," she croaked.

"Ew," agreed Chris Hevans.

Bev and Gorm the Vicious echoed their "Ew," and even the dead man's hand seemed disgusted, flicking Fenris's inner goop off its fingers.

Mott's right hand was empty. She'd lost Odin's eye.

But when she opened her left hand she almost cried with relief. The Rune of Annihilation rested in her palm.

Something wet and rough licked her cheek, and she found herself staring into the face of a dirty, tiny wolf pup.

"Mweep?"

"Good boy, Fenris, good boy," she said, scritching his chin.

Dizzy and wobbly, she got to her feet.

"Mott, over here!" Mott's mother was cowering with Hermod behind a big concrete planter. Broken glass glittered amid pulverized bricks and the wreckage of demolished shops. Snowing ash continued to fall.

"Good to see you back, friend Mott!" shouted Thrudi over the clang of her blade against Tew's ax. "As you can see, the battle goes well."

Despite her jaunty tone, Thrudi was not, in fact, doing well. Blood striped her cheeks, one of her arms hung awkwardly at her side, and she moved with a limp. Tew and Vidar easily dodged her attempts to cut and stab and slice them.

She wouldn't last much longer.

Mott thrust her hand in the air. "Stop!" she shouted. "I have the rune." She opened her hand to show them. The annihilation symbol shone like a lamp in the dark.

Vidar and Tew paused. Exhausted, Thrudi sank to one knee and tried to catch her breath.

"You do, indeed, have the rune," Vidar said, his voice mild. "That is a feat worthy of song."

Tew appraised her as if he were trying to decide how to carve a turkey. "I guess we take it from her and shove it back down Fenris's throat?"

Vidar considered for a moment. "I suppose so. He no longer looks so hungrily at the moon. And he *does* have to eat the moon before he can kill Odin, and only then can I kill him."

The two gods were calm. They were unhurt and looked fresh. Thrudi had done her part. The rest was up to Mott.

The rune wasn't much bigger than a cookie. She placed it between her teeth.

"You wouldn't dare," said Tew. But he didn't sound too certain.

Mott aimed a defiant smile at him.

"You don't know where that thing's been," said Mott's mom in a stern mom voice. "Spit it out right now."

Mott's smile turned apologetic.

Thrudi gazed at her, eyes shining, face grimy with soot and blood. She understood what Mott was going to do, and the admiration in her expression was beautifully clear.

"You have the heart of a Valkyrie, sister."

Mott beamed.

Vidar turned even whiter. Frost billowed around him

with every breath. He pointed the tip of his sword right at the center of Mott's chest. "So you eat the rune and then what? You are seized with the desire to destroy? You gain power and you finish what Fenris started and ravage the moon? Then the sun?"

"Maybe this is how the prophecy plays out," Tew suggested. "The girl brings the moon down to Earth in pieces, Fenris eats the crumbs, events continue as promised, and the prophecy is preserved."

"Buh wah if ah jush bide it im two?" said Mott, her words garbled by the rune in her mouth.

"I didn't understand that." Vidar looked around for help. "Did anyone understand that?"

Thrudi translated for him. "She said, 'But what if I just bite it in two?'"

"Ih wud refweef a forf lig a nookweer bob."

"It would—" began Thrudi.

"Release a force like a nuclear bomb," Tew finished. "You'd flatten every building, cook every plant to cinders, kill every living creature within a few dozen miles, and poison the air and the water and the land for thousands of lifetimes. We all know you're not going to do that."

"Mebee ah will."

"You wouldn't!" Mott's mom said, scandalized. "You're a good girl." She turned to the gods. "Don't mind my daughter. She's bluffing."

Mott shifted the rune in her mouth just enough that she could speak more clearly. "You're not helping, Mom."

There was an edge of regret in Vidar's voice. "You're just prolonging the worlds' pain. Delaying this further is simply cruel. Stop it. Give us the rune, and let's end this tragedy."

"Mweep," said Fenris.

Tew brought his ax up high. Red blood glowed beneath his flesh. Vidar gripped his sword in both his hands. His eyes steamed with frost. Once more, Mott's balance faltered and her brain wobbled with the Grand Canyon sensation.

"You made too many promises," Tew said, with some sympathy. "And you are out of options."

"That's not true." Mott gathered the last remnants of her courage. She gathered her strength, drawn from Thrudi and her mom and Fenris, and from the certainty that everyone depended on her now.

From Thrudi's bag, which lay on the ground, she grabbed a bottle of Borbles root beer.

She popped the bottle open.

She pushed the rune onto her tongue and closed her mouth.

She took a swig.

"Don't you do it," whispered Vidar. "Don't you eat that rune."

Mott did it.

Mott ate that rune.

She felt . . . different.

Not bad.

Not good.

Just hugely different.

She took a step.

It was just a step. Nothing threatening in it, nothing special.

Tew and Vidar watched her, their weapons ready, their eyes narrowed, and their muscles clenched. Thrudi moved to put herself between Mott and the gods, but Mott waved her off. "I'll be okay."

Mott wasn't actually sure that she would be okay. If the gods hurt Thrudi, Mott wasn't sure what she would do, or what she would become. And anyway, this wasn't a fight that could be won with swords and axes.

She brought her foot down lightly on the pavement, and a little cloud of ash poofed in the air. There was a soft crunch, like the cracking ice film of a mug of root beer from the back of the fridge. When she lifted her foot, there was a tiny fissure in the concrete.

"Okay," she said. "Okay."

She drove her foot down again, harder this time, and the ground cracked like an eggshell. A shudder vibrated through the earth.

Tew flinched. Not a lot, but it was a definite flinch. She had just made a god of war flinch.

"Have you ever seen the Grand Canyon?" she asked him.

"No."

"It's a little bit like this."

She opened her mouth and roared. She roared the immense power of the rune inside her. She roared all her fear, and she roared all her anger, but mostly she roared her love and she roared her resolve to keep her promises.

The air shook with the sound of a mighty horn, a tuba the size of a volcano, a choir of jet engines, a symphony of freight trains. Mott was shocked and frightened when she realized the sound came from her.

Tew and Vidar covered their ears and staggered, trying to stay on their feet while hurricane winds tore at their atoms.

She was a black hole.

She was emptiness.

She was devastation.

She was the death of worlds.

She was Ragnarok.

If she wanted to be.

She shut her mouth, and the gods collapsed to the pavement. They lay there, breathing hard and softly moaning.

After a while, Tew recovered the ability to speak. "Yes, you're powerful," he panted. "Now, instead of Fenris being my weapon, it can be you. Do you feel the rage inside? The pressure, like two seismic plates pushing against each other, like magma boiling under your skin?" He pointed at the moon in the sky. "Do it, girl. Become your greatest self and fulfill the destiny you robbed from Fenris. Fulfill the prophecy's promise."

Mott had a choice.

Not like the move to Los Angeles. Not like her mom losing the job she'd been promised. Not like living in an apartment complex with a no-dogs policy. Not like having a dad who lied as easily as Loki.

"Are you kidding?" Mott said. "I'm not going to eat an entire moon. I made a promise to save Fenris." She looked at the two gods, two big men, crawling on the ground. She almost felt sorry for them. "And I promised to save the worlds."

She parted her lips and let out just a tiny bit more of her Grand Canyon might. Compared to her previous roar, it was hardly a wheeze.

Vidar put his hands up in surrender. "Enough."

"Enough? What do you mean, 'Enough'?" Tew snorted. "We don't get to give up. We don't get to decide if Ragnarok happens or not." He gestured at Thrudi and Mott's mom and Chris Hevans and all the other bystanders. "Gods we may be, but compared to the universe, we're as small as they are to us. We do our part to fulfill the prophecy, and we can do nothing else."

Wincing, Vidar stood.

"Yes, my brother-in-arms. You are correct. Ragnarok will happen. The promise of death to all worlds will be kept. The world-spanning serpent will thrash beneath the waves and drown the land. The flaming sword of Surtur will turn worlds to ash. Fenris will eat the moon. There will be an age of axes, and an age of swords, and an age of wolves, till the worlds go down." He offered his hand to Tew and lifted him to his feet. "But not today." Vidar dipped his chin in a small bow to Mott. "You have shown courage, and you have my respect."

"I don't want your respect," Mott said.

Vidar allowed himself a smile.

"Come, Tew. Let's go home. We will rest and feast, and we will prepare for the next final tomorrow."

Scowling, Tew hefted his ax over his shoulder. "Very well, brother. Until the final tomorrow." And aiming a glare at Mott, he said, "Which may come much sooner than you think."

Together, the gods shuffled out of the mall, leaving rubble and ruin behind.

"You better run!" shouted Chris Hevans, long after they had gone.

Mott wasn't sure how she felt. Relieved? Proud? Or just exhausted? Thrudi came to her side, and they leaned on each other. "Should we go after them, friend Thrudi?"

"That sounds like a very stupid idea, friend Mott. But if you wish, I will stand with you."

Smoke still billowed in the red sky. Mounds of broken glass and brick and cement still sprawled all around them. Helicopters labored in the air and sirens wailed.

"Let them go," Mott said. "There's work to do here."

Fenris toddled over and booped Mott's leg until she picked him up.

"Mweep," he said in total agreement.

17

SCIENTISTS TOOK MEASUREMENTS AND DID math and calculated how much of the moon had been lost. Most of the crumbs had fallen in the ocean, some in a remote Mongolian desert, one in the middle of an empty football stadium in Florida, and a lot of the crumbs burned up in the atmosphere before striking ground. Earth was lucky there weren't more crumbs and that the crumbs weren't bigger.

But that didn't mean Almost-Ragnarok hadn't done a lot of harm. The fires in Hollywood destroyed homes. Bigger fires in Australia burned millions of acres. Floods in India took lives, and even now, in the middle of summer, parts of Europe grappled with a strange winter storm. Los Angeles was still as warm and dry as the inside of a toaster and felt ready to burst into flames again.

Mott didn't know how much Almost-Ragnarok was to blame for the deadly weather and how much was due to stuff people had been doing for more than a century: the products built in factories and shipped across oceans, the things power plants burned to generate electricity. It didn't take a prophecy to break a world.

Things done could not be undone. Things destroyed could not be undestroyed. But sometimes they could be fixed. Tomorrow Mott was volunteering to help clean up storm debris on the beach. The day after that, she was going to the library to talk about starting a neighborhood environmental sustainability club.

She knew she had power. Maybe not the power to get her mom a better-paying job. Or the power to change the apartment's anti-dog policy. But she had power to make things better. She supposed everybody did.

For now she sat on the couch with Thrudi, watching the end credits of a Chris Hevans movie.

"He's actually a good actor," Mott judged. "Four out of five bubbles."

The dead man's hand sat on Thrudi's shoulder, reaching for the popcorn. "I agree, though I think a human sacrifice would have improved the story. Want some?"

Thrudi offered Mott popcorn, but the dead man's hand had put her off her appetite. Instead she gave it to the hamster on her knee, who happily munched it.

"How sits the rune within you?" Thrudi asked. "Do you yet feel an urge to annihilate?"

"Not really? I feel . . . strong? And weird?"

"Then perhaps the rune was poorly named. There are sources of wisdom in the other worlds—libraries, lore keepers, lords of secrets—and they may have knowledge that might better help us understand the power you possess. I will visit them for you, and if I find answers, I will share them with you. I promise."

"You really can't stay?" The last few days had been so horrible, and the future looked scary, but one part of it was so good: she'd met Thrudi, who was closer than Mott's own siblings, the closest friend Mott had ever had.

Thrudi smiled sadly. "The harm wrought on your world was also wrought on mine. If you're going to repair things here, I must help repair things there. You would think less of me if I didn't."

"Another Chris Hevans movie first?"

Thrudi gasped in delighted surprise. "There are more?"

"I'll put on the one where he's an archaeologist. Oh, I think there may be human sacrifice in that one."

Thrudi settled back into the cushions. "Finally, a story worthy of Valkyries! Press Play!"

Hours later, they stood in the alley behind the apartment building. Thrudi sat on Scooty with a six-pack of Burppenpaup root beer in her bag, the very best root beer Mott had ever reviewed, earning ten of five bubbles. The dead man's hand sat on her shoulder, playing with a lock of her hair.

Mott coughed to clear the lump in her throat. "How does this work? You ride off into the sunset?"

Thrudi tightened the strap on her bag. "It would be a very long ride to my world. No, I will leave the same way I arrived. With this."

She showed Mott the rune in her hand. It was the same size as the Annihilation Rune, but etched with a different symbol.

"Do you . . . do you have to eat it?"

"Do you eat a key before you put it in a lock?"

"Nope."

"Well, then." She drew a circle in the air with the rune. The air shimmered, forming an arc that stretched out into the far distance, dancing with all the colors of the rainbow and other colors that seemed at the very edge of Mott's ability to see.

"This is the Bifrost," Thrudi said. "The bridge between the roots of the World Tree. The path to my world is straight ahead."

Mott sniffed. "So, I guess this is it."

Thrudi swallowed. Her eyes shone. "You be good, Fenris, son of Loki," she said, gently rubbing a fingernail down the back of the hamster riding on Mott's shoulder. The hamster yawned a little yawn. "And you," she said to Mott, "you use this whenever you need."

She placed the rune key in Mott's hand.

"What if I need it next week?"

Thrudi laughed. "That long?"

She took a breath, started Scooty's motor, and put-putted her way down the bridge.

Mott watched her until she was too far to see, and she didn't turn away until the colors faded, returning the air to normal.

Mott put the hamster on the ground and appraised the garbage-strewn alley. "Lots of work to do, shape-changer," she said to the blue-eyed, white-furred wolf. "Wanna help?"

The wolf pup blepped his tongue at her. "Mweep."

ACKNOWLEDGMENTS

Just as Mott faces her daunting tasks with the assistance of the brave and mighty Thrudi, I had a lot of help turning my stack of words into a proper book and getting it into your hands. I owe thanks to the following awesome people: Erica Sussman and Stephanie Guerdan for their tireless work and keen editorial minds; Deanna Hoak, the best copyeditor in the business; Mitchell Thorpe, the finest of publicists; Jessica Berg for additional sharp-eyed editing; Vivienne To for her extraordinary cover and Chris Kwon for his gorgeous design; and the many, many HarperCollins team members whose work behind the scenes in sales, marketing, administration, and other departments deserves abundant praise and appreciation.

My thanks to the brilliant Holly Root, a true champion, and Alyssa Moore for a thousand unseen tasks, including telling folks about my book on Root Literary's social media accounts.

Thank you to the many dozens of librarians, teachers, booksellers, book enthusiasts, friends, acquaintances, and complete strangers who generously put their energies into helping authors like me.

I can never fully express my gratitude to Lisa Will, without whom I simply could not devote as much energy as I do to writing and to whom this book, my tenth published novel, is dedicated, as was my very first.

Finally, I want to acknowledge and thank the many scientists, science communicators, teachers, activists, public servants, and everyday people of all ages who are fighting to prevent the very real Ragnarok of human-caused climate change.